A CASE OF DOMESTIC PILFERING

A Case Of Domestic Pilfering

Rohase Piercy
with
Charlie Raven

This is a work of fiction. Any resemblance to persons living or dead is purely coincidental.

A Case Of Domestic Pilfering
Copyright © 2017 Rohase Piercy
All rights reserved.

No part of this text may be used or reproduced in any form, except for the inclusion of brief quotations in review, without written permission from the author.

Cover Design by Katie Alexander

ISBN: 1539782204
ISBN-13: 978-1539782209

This story was conceived and written down by its original author, Charlie Raven, in 1987. I am extremely grateful to have been granted the privilege of editing and adapting it – a thoroughly enjoyable process – and presenting it for publication in its present form.

Rohase Piercy

Louis ...

Monsieur Louis la Rothière hummed a merry air to himself as he tied the stiff cambric into a bow at his neck. Just a *soupcon* of parfum de toilette ... there. Like a delicate breeze in the room. He would pause at the door, the footman would announce him, faces would turn; he would smile...

His mild, watery blue eyes studied his reflection in the glass as he carefully combed his moustache. He'd tried side whiskers a while ago, but had found them ageing; and too *English*. It was important to strike the right note.

Downstairs, he sat back in his armchair and lit a cigar, pleased to contemplate the effect of evening sunshine through stained glass. He'd grown fond of these lodgings, he realised. He'd be sorry if it became necessary to leave, especially with so much yet to accomplish. Business was – not good exactly, but getting better. With this latest opportunity, it might really take off. And how pleasant it would be to pull off a coup while everyone else was out of town!

He glanced furtively towards the fireplace and thought lovingly of his latest cache, concealed beneath a brick in the grate. How satisfying to know that those sheets were there, covered in their diagrams and formulae! Undoubtedly an impressive treatise, but requiring an expert to assess its value .. Louis frowned, and thought with less pleasure of the fee he would have to find for that service; but one could not approach one's contacts without knowing the market value of one's wares.

And there might be more where that came from. Most satisfactory.

He supposed it was nearly time to go; one must not keep dear Mrs Carnforth waiting, and she had been most insistent that he arrive early. It would be a colourful party, and as an unattached gentleman Louis would be at a premium. There was that, of course – the tedious dancing with wallflowers to please la belle Carnforth – but it was a small price to pay for an entree to an establishment where he could expect to pick up many nuggets. A French accent and a knowing air could charm the most chilly of dowagers, and Louis knew exactly the note to touch. How they prattled away when flattered!

He filled his cigarette case, and tucked some cigars away for later. He saw himself smoking on the balcony overlooking the Park, music drifting through open windows while he inclined a sympathetic ear to some murmured confidence, or listened covertly to a useful conversation. He had, incidentally, made quite sure that the French attache would not, after all, be present; he had no intention of attempting conversation with a real French national.

Louis turned down the gas. He did not keep a servant for security reasons; his chambers were cleaned by the Greek widow who took care of his washing. Her English was poor, but he had managed to charm her - had taken care to charm her, as a fellow emigre - and she was fiercely loyal. She would defend any irregularity in his lifestyle if questioned, banding with him against the foreign city where life was so hard and at the same time so dull. She was a conquest too, in a way. All stations in life interested him.

He closed the front door carefully, checking the latch before lightly descending the front steps. He smiled to himself as he crossed the street to the cab rank. Louis la Rothière, he reflected, was quite the chameleon.

Guy and Max ...

Mr Guy Clements' drawing room was a symphony in the modern style. He had employed a talented designer to oversee its décor; two talented designers, in fact, for an unfortunate disagreement had arisen between himself and his first choice, necessitating the summoning of a second Talent ... by which time Guy had rather lost interest. The room had suffered little, and only in respect of the first designer's fascination with Chinoiserie and the second's with Moorish design. Guy carried off the clash with confidence, being a young man of considerable charm and cheerful disposition. Guests were rarely left to contemplate the effect of Moroccan lamp on Ming vase.

He was sitting now in the warm glow of an August evening, sending puffs of cigarette smoke up to the ceiling and talking incessantly. His feet were drawn up on the divan and one elbow rested on an immense sausage of a cushion.

'So you can see how tedious it's been, Maxy, here on my own all these months and months. I couldn't stay with Mother – all those never-ending tea-parties and dinner parties with hundreds of unremarkable young women twittering aimlessly... and they all have enormous, formidable Mamas! They really quite frighten me! I shock them though; I avenge myself for the tedium.'

'*Do* you shock them?' His guest was sitting in a chair whose legs took the form of a writhing, black-lacquered dragon. His brown eyes were thoughtful, his dark hair dishevelled, and he looked tired; he'd had a long journey on a hot afternoon, and Guy had not stopped talking for the last half-hour. The two young men were of an age, but a more serous nature and a reticent manner made Max appear older than his twenty-one years.

'Of course I shock them! You know Maxy, the people I've been meeting recently are not like anybody you'd encounter down in Sussex. They're artistic, they write novels, they know actresses. And when one's milieu is the *vie de Boheme,* it does tend to seep into conversation.'

'I thought you said life had been tedious without me!'

'Well of course it was tedious without *you.'* Guy smiled charmingly. 'That's why you're here, because it's all utterly *pointless* without *you.'*

Max looked dubious. As he toyed with the empty glass in his hand, his eye fell upon a tall blue-glazed vase standing guard upon the mantelpiece.

'Is that Chinese?' he asked, indicating it with the glass. 'All those writhing dragons… it could be a priceless antique!'

'Oh loads of this stuff is antique,' said Guy happily. 'You can just feel it, can't you, all those centuries here in this room. It makes me go quite quiet from time to time ... oh, how utterly remiss of me! Your glass is empty! Do let me help you to another.'

Guy rose, and went over to the decanter on the sideboard. 'You know, Maxy,' he continued. 'I haven't really been living the *vie de Boheme*. I've been been quite reclusive some of the time. I've been reading a lot - you'd be pleased. There's one book I've just finished, about a ghastly murder which -'

'Don't spoil the plot for me!' cried Max.

'No no, of course not. Except it's all set somewhere in Sussex, with this gruesome old chap who reminded me so much of your father that I thought you should read it. He's the murderer. The gruesome old chap, I mean, not your father. Here.'

'Thanks.' Max accepted the proffered glass, and sipped. Tiredness was giving way to a slight, pleasant wooziness. Having run through Guy's new fads, the confirmation that they were really the old fads after all was heartening. They were drifting back into intimacy, and Max was suddenly filled with affection for the foolish room and its jumbled treasures. He smiled as he watched his friend ease himself gracefully back onto the divan.

'But Maxy, you've been awfully quiet. I could almost believe you've got a secret. What is it? Or should I say, *who* is it? Some rustic farm boy?' Guy tittered gently.

Max sighed indulgently. 'I've been quiet because I couldn't get a word in edgeways!'

'How unkind! Go on then. The floor is yours. Tell me all about him.'

'There is no 'him'. Don't smirk like that. If you

want to know, I *have* been leading a tedious reclusive life, all alone with Father in that horrible house. I wish he'd get rid of it, the place is falling to bits, but he clings on, getting more miserable and miserly by the year. Your invitation was a release from prison, I can tell you.'

'Yes, and it had Mother's full approval! She likes you, which can't be said for all my friends unfortunately.'

'I know she likes me.'

'Yes. She does. Another cigarette? They're Alexandrian, all the way from Morocco.'

Guy proffered his case and Max extracted a cigarette gingerly, regarding it with suspicion. 'These aren't packed with opium, are they?'

'No!' said Guy, surprised. 'Did you think they might be?'

'I thought it might account for the smell ...'

'Smell? It's an exotic perfume!'

'Like fish ...'

'It is not like fish!'

'It is. And Alexandria is not in -'

A well-aimed cushion ended the remark. When the ensuing tussle was over, they composed themselves and addressed the question of dinner. It transpired that Guy had made no arrangements with Cook except that sandwiches would be awaiting their return.

'We'll have to eat out then,' said Max thoughtfully. He began to worry that his small purse would not outlast his stay. Guy enjoyed a personal fortune, inherited from his late father upon his coming of age; even as an undergraduate he'd had difficulty grasping the fact that money was an exhaustible commodity. Tonight however, to Max's relief, he suggested a quiet, inexpensive restaurant.

'Well, we want to be intimate, don't we?' smiled Guy, pinching his arm. 'A whole month, Maxy! The longest month ever. Just you and me together, with the whole of London at our feet. Isn't it glorious?'

An hour or so later, Max sat by his friend's bedroom window looking out at the dark square nestled beneath a glowing indigo sky. The thrown-up sash let in cool, scented air.

'Is that a nightingale? Listen...'

'Oh, probably.' Guy was fussing with his necktie in front of the mirror. 'Maxy, remind me to discuss some things with you later. Really important things.'

'Things. All right. I will.'

'Yes. Ready? How do I look?'

'Divine, as always. And I've been ready for the last half-hour.'

'Off we go then. The purple night beckons!'

They descended the stairs together, laughing.

Madeleine and Michael ...

Madeleine had been stooping, picking at the flattened granules of something ground into the carpet. Now she straightened, red in the face, and sat back on her heels for a moment until a movement at the door made her jump.

'Only me!'

Madeleine turned away. 'So I see. How come you always turn up when the work's half finished?'

'It was John. He kept me to help with – to help him shift something.' The older girl moved across the room slowly, humming.

'Well, you took your time. I've already cleaned over there, by the way.'

'So you have. Good little worker, ain't you Mary? Shall I do over here then?'

My name is not Mary, protested Madeleine silently. 'No need. It's all done, Sarah.'

'Well, lemme carry that then. Oh by the way – ain't it your half day today? Don't feel like swapping with me by any chance? I got some things I want to do.'

'No, I don't. I've got things to do as well.'

'Oh come on, Mary! What things?' Sarah sat down on the piano stool; the lid was up, and she ran a finger along the keys.

'Sush that! They'll hear you!'

'Not them. They didn't get in 'till light. I heard

'em.'

'Couldn't sleep, eh?'

Sarah ignored the dig. 'You're mean, you are, Mary,' she said in complaining tones. 'You get much more fun than me, living out like you do. It's work, work, work here, all day long.'

'*I* work. Or hadn't you noticed?' *And my name is not Mary.*

'Well, I'd have thought you could do me just one tiny favour...'

'I'm always doing you favours.' Madeleine made toward the door. '*I've* got things to do,' she repeated over her shoulder.

'Must be love, then!' laughed Sarah as she slid from the piano stool.

Madeleine stood still for a moment. 'No,' she said firmly; 'No, it's not love.'

They crossed the hall in silence, and disappeared down the back stairs.

Later, she threaded her way through the crowd. It was hot, and although she'd washed her face and hands before leaving Mr Clements' house she felt dirty and sticky. The pavements burned through the soles of her shoes, and the smell of people, horses and hot tar invaded her nose. At last she decided to blow some wages on an omnibus, rummaging in her purse to find the requisite coppers.

Home at last, tired and flushed, feeling the hair cling damply to her forehead, she ascended the three steps and opened the door. Immediately the smell of cabbage puffed at her, accompanied by its auditory equivalent: Mr Morgan's voice lessons wafting down the stairwell. She hurried into the back room she shared with her mother, pulling at the ribbons of her bonnet.

Her mother was in bed, a great heap under the covers, snoring. The yellow blinds trapped the air; the room smelled of sweat and unwashed linen. Madeleine wrinkled her nose, withdrawing quietly. She went downstairs to the basement where her younger brother Michael was reading at the kitchen table.

'Is that tea?' She sat down opposite him as he refilled the cup at his elbow and pushed it towards her.

'What you reading, Mikey?'

He held up the book. *'The Terrible Fate of Lady Melrose,'* she read aloud. 'That's the same one you were reading last week!'

'Yeah. It's got some good bits in it. This Lady gets kidnapped by a gang of roughs - here, look -'

Madeleine read curiously. 'That's *rude'*. She pushed the book away, blushing involuntarily.

Michael was grinning. 'I don't mind.'

'Don't suppose you do. Anyway, no-one talks like that in real life.' She swept some biscuit crumbs aside.

'It's books, innit? Anyway, I'll be getting a new one tomorrow because – look.' He slid something into his palm and made a fist. 'Which one?'

'That one.' He opened his hand.

'Well well,' she said softly. 'You *have* been earning your keep now, haven't you?' She looked at him. 'Anything else?'

'No. Straightforward, this one. Never seen him before – new to it, by the looks of him.'

Madeleine nodded. 'It's the regulars who turn out more interesting from my point of view.'

'And mine. Did your Frog go for those papers?'

'Difficult to tell, but he was interested all right. Enough to make your gent worth another squeeze.'

'I'll squeeze him all right. They're pathetic, that sort – dead scared, but keep coming back for more. Must be my charm.' Michael smiled pleasantly. 'The price'll go up this time, though. We could do some serious business – tell your Frog that. By the by, what about *your* gent? Any chance there?'

'Mr Clements? Too risky. Anyway, he's catered for. Got a nice friend staying with him now.'

'One of us?' Michael leaned forward, interested.

'Nah. He sticks to his own.'

Michael sat in silence for a while; Madeleine watched him. He met her eyes.

'Mads - d'you think I should buy something for Ma with this?' Suddenly he looked very young.

'She never notices! Don't know why you bother.'

'Don't be hard on her, Mads. She can't help it.'

'I'm sick of hearing that.' Madeleine spoke coldly. 'She has it easy compared to you. And me.'

'She's had a deal of trouble …'

'We've all got trouble. Don't get soft on me, Mikey. You won't last if you're soft.'

'I think I know that better than you,' said Michael quietly. 'Don't be angry Mads.'

There was a pause. 'When you seeing him, then? Your Frog?'

'Dunno. Tonight, maybe. Or maybe not. I'm tired.' She rubbed her eyes and passed a hand through her dirty yellow hair. 'No, tonight. I could do with a run. It helps.'

'I know,' said Michael.

Upstairs Mrs Peterson reached a crescendo of snores, and on the floor above Mr Morgan's pupil trilled on top G, cracked, and gamely tried again. 'Bravo!' came his voice, drifting faintly down the stairs; 'Bravo!'

Max and Guy ...

'*W*hat?'

'I think you heard me. I articulated with considerable precision,' drawled Guy. He was smoking, and playing with his watch chain.

'You bloody fool!' Max marched to the window. He stood with his hands thrust into his pockets, compressing his lips.

'Oh, language, dear Max.'

'How on earth could you do something so utterly stupid?' hissed Max, apparently addressing a lady in a large summer hat as she strolled past the railings. 'Well, how?' He swung round. 'Answer me, Guy!'

'Oh, I thought you were being rhetorical. You're ever so good at that.'

'You are an absolute bloody fool!'

Guy closed his eyes and rested his head on the back of the chair. One leg swung over the arm, the pointed shiny shoe beating time to an inaudible tune. He sighed noisily.

'It was necessary, that's all. *Necessitas mater inventorum est, n'est-ce pas?*'

'But couldn't it *wait*? It's nearly the end of the quarter!'

'That's exactly what I told *him*! But the wretched man insists on harassing me with reminders, and interest rates and so forth. So tedious.' Guy opened his eyes. 'Don't be brutish, Maxy. Mother never wears the silly things anyway, and they'll be back with her in no time. No harm, no repercussions. Anyway-' he began to snigger - 'That's not the funniest thing.'

'I don't see that any of it is *funny*.'

'The funniest thing,' grinned Guy swinging round to sit forwards in his chair, 'Is that they're practically worthless.'

'Eh?'

Guy nodded, his blue eyes sparkling. 'Paste, apparently. A hundred was all I could get for them. It's kept the old boy happy though – a little down payment, and he'll get the rest at the end of next month. Actually, if I'd known he'd be happy with a mere hundred I needn't have gone to all that trouble!'

'So – you've pawned your mother's jewellery unnecessarily, and you're still in debt.'

'And darling Mother has a skeleton revealed. *Voila!* An ancient, dry old mummy – I mean skeleton – *dans le cabinet.*'

Max could not help smiling at his friend's inexhaustible spirits. He was bubbling with naughtiness.

'How do you know it reveals any such thing?'

'Of course it does! My stepfather goes on and on about those tedious bourgeois rocks. Its obvious that Mother's done a little conjuring trick at some point in her chequered career.'

'Well it may not have been her ...' Max went to sit opposite Guy and regarded him closely. 'It could have been Sir Edward.'

'He wouldn't. My step-papa simply would not have the imagination to play such a trick. He'd go up in my estimation if he did, I assure you!'

'Oh well.' Max sighed and rubbed his forehead. 'As you say, so long as you get the things back before anyone misses them ... But look here, why didn't you just go to your mother and ask for an advance?'

'Such a thing would not be possible. My independent allowance seems to annoy all right-thinking members of my family as it is, and she'd be bound to ask questions. I'm not quite *au fait* with the details, dear boy, but apparently Papa put in some kind of clause, or appendage or whatever it is, to prevent his only son and heir from running full tilt through his generous leavings. If I show signs of 'bad financial management' - or even signs of enjoying myself too much - then snap! The steel jaws close around the bank and I am sent off to shoot grouse in the country or something dreadful like that.'

'I see. Probably a good thing too,' growled Max.

'Oh Maxy. You do put things so baldly. I hope this baldness won't begin to manifest itself physically.'

'Shut up, Guy. I'm trying to think.'

'Boasting again ...' Guy rose and came over to make a thorough inspection of Max's hairline.

'Look. Stop pestering me. You can be most provoking. Sit down, Guy!'

Max sprung up and pushed his friend backwards into the armchair. Guy froze into a pretty pose.

'Seriously. Listen. You're telling me that having

pawned your mother's necklace behind her back, you're still in debt to a moneylender?'

'Spot on.'

'How much?'

'H'mm, h'mm …' Guy cupped his hand round his lips and mouthed a figure.

'My God!'

'Don't tell *Him!'* Guy pointed a white finger to the heavens. 'The great Accountant in the sky. Not in my good books. His fault anyway.'

'And why should that be, now?'

'Sure, 'twas the nag I backed. I'd have plenty left in the kitty if I hadn't slapped the lot on.'

'One horse?'

'One or two or five. Oh, it was a fateful, golden afternoon, Maxy. The champagne flowed like wine - it is wine, in fact - and I couldn't tell how many horses. A charming fellow got into conversation with me - quite charming …'

'Oh yes?'

'Yes! He was ever so knowledgeable about the turf and all things turfy. Convivial, helpful, gave me a few tips. There we are. Never seen the fellow since. To be honest Maxy, I can't remember what tips he gave me. Neither can I remember whether I took his advice. He just inspired me, in a general manner, and I felt moved, positively moved, to try my luck.'

'You were trying to impress him,' said Max in his severest tone.

'Oh, I did impress. I feel sure of that. But when I came back, there he wasn't. Sad ending.'

'All too common in these dark days, I fear.'

'How true.' Guy stretched. 'Look, let's go out. Let's go and call on my charming *Maman* and drink tea in her cool green drawing room. She likes you, Maxy. She thinks you're sensible, and a good influence.'

'Yes. I know. I am. And I like her. But I don't think I could quite face her this afternoon, after what you've just told me; I'd get all tongue-tied, and start bringing diamonds and paste and skeletons into the conversation for no reason.'

'Oh God, Maxy, you mustn't! Oh, why do you have to be such a compulsive truth-teller? I shall never be able to trust you with Mother again!'

'You will, you will. I'll be the soul of discretion. Just not this afternoon. It's too soon.'

'The park, then. A stroll in the park, followed by a drink of something cool and decadent. Oh come on, Maxy. Forget about all that tedious money business. It'll be paid off at the end of next month, and Mother will get her fake diamonds back and be none the wiser. I know it's hot, but -'

Max got up. 'Shall we?'

'Oh. Yes, do let's.' Guy rose gracefully, and took his arm.

Holmes and Watson ...

Baker Street was like an oven. The August sun glanced off the facades of the houses, and the road shimmered. The street was busy with traffic, but horses and humans were moving at half their accustomed pace.

Dr Watson sat at the window overlooking the street, glancing down at the scene below from time to time as though seeking inspiration there. Before him lay a thick pad of yellow foolscap, one page half covered with his small, neat handwriting. The rest of the table was littered with scribbled notes.

'Holmes?' he said without turning round, 'When was it you said that those singular events had been set in motion – relating, you know, to the Grice-Pattersons?'

'Not that one, if you please, my dear fellow,' came the languid response from the couch. 'There, I fear, we must exercise a little discretion. The full story may have certain repercussions, and even a skilful account could not disguise the identity of that well-known member of the French government.'

Dr Watson twisted round to look at his companion. 'I hope you are not implying that my account would be lacking in skill?' he smiled sweetly at the figure lounging in the dim room.

'Not for the world, my dear Watson,' murmured Sherlock Holmes listlessly.

Dr Watson sighed, and turned back to his pad. 'Then it must be the unfortunate Mr Openshaw.'

His companion said nothing, but Watson heard him strike a match to light his pipe. The acrid smoke curled across the room and reached him at the window.

'My dear Holmes!' he protested, 'There's hardly enough air in here as it is. I beg you to leave us just a little to breathe.'

He stood up and pulled at the sash; immediately the noise of voices, feet and traffic entered the room, along with a puff of stale air. He sat down again and pushed back the hair from his forehead with a capable brown hand. Then he sighed, and threw down his pen.

'No good,' he said, wandering across to his armchair.

Holmes glanced abstractedly at him, and returned to his perusal of The Times agony column. Around his couch, the somewhat threadbare carpet was littered with newspapers; a scattering of cigarette ends and matches, scissors, glue pot, ink bottle and pens lay on the table. On the chairs themselves lay a variety of miscellaneous objects such as chemical pipettes, sheet music and scraps of paper covered in jottings, the import of which would presumably be clear to Holmes but certainly to nobody else. The mantelpiece differed from the rest of the chaos only by the presence of a large jackknife skewering a sheaf of papers at its centre; why these papers should be thus honoured became apparent when inspection revealed them to be unpaid bills and unanswered correspondence.

Dr Watson's eyes wandered to the bills, and he sighed. He sat for a moment, making half-hearted calculations relating to his own finances and giving up as his arithmetic succumbed to the enervating heat.

'What are your plans today, Holmes?' he asked in a desultory attempt to alleviate his own boredom.

'H'mmm?'

'Got a case to work on?'

'You know I have not.' Holmes suddenly shuffled the newspaper together and tossed it onto the floor. He stretched and yawned. 'Nothing,' he said bleakly; 'Nothing whatever to do.' He fixed his grey eyes on the wall and lay back motionless on the couch. His friend noted the dull, lack-lustre gaze and pallid face, and his own kind blue eyes grew troubled.

'Come for a walk, my dear fellow?' he asked pleasantly.

Holmes did not answer. He closed his eyes and compressed his lips.

'Nothing,' he said bitterly. 'I shall go mad soon, Watson.'

'Come for a walk instead,' said Watson good-humouredly, watching the thin face closely.

'Leave me alone.'

Watson rose, unperturbed. 'Well then *I* shall go for a walk. I have no intention of being cooped up with someone in imminent danger of going mad. I think I shall take a pleasant stroll along to the park. Then I shall have a cool hock-and-seltzer. H'mmm?'

There was no reaction. Dr Watson quietly slipped a small bottle of colourless liquid from the mantelpiece into his pocket as he made his way to the door.

'Put it back, Watson. This minute,' came the incisive voice.

Watson sighed, and replaced it. Holmes was apparently satisfied, for he maintained a moody silence and closed his eyes while Watson skilfully conveyed the Morocco case containing a hypodermic syringe into his pocket and went on his way, whistling ostentatiously.

... and now, the game's afoot!

The park was cool in the shade. The huge trees exhaled a faint green aroma, sweet and calm. Max and Guy had stopped together, looking across the scorched grass to where white parasols and floating silhouettes passed like a mirage in the sunlight.

'Hot, isn't it?' said Guy taking off his hat. The hair was dark on his glistening forehead. Max fanned him with his hat rim.

'It's just as well we're not going to your mother's,' he said. 'It's too hot to be out at all, really. I vote we gather ourselves for a quick sprint across the grass to an arbour of refreshment, and deal with a couple of ice-cold hock-and-seltzers.'

'I second that,' murmured Guy. He leaned ostentatiously against the tree, closed his eyes and muttered 'Water, water – I mean, hock, hock-and-seltzer!'

In his light suit and straw hat he should be on the river, thought Max. In a punt. Just he and I. Cool, green, glassy waters. He put out a hand and quietly touched his arm.

'Guy.'

Guy opened his eyes and smiled. He has the face of a Sun God, thought Max.

'Guy, you look just like Phoebus Apollo.'

Guy glanced quickly round. 'Oh Maxy, you are

sweet. If I'm Apollo then who can you be? Daphne?'

They both shouted with laughter as they walked arm in arm into the sunlight.

Inside the bar the air was cool. A breeze slid through the open windows, and the waiters looked clean in their starched white aprons. Max was sitting back, trying not to scrutinise his own reflection in the enormous gilt mirror on the opposite wall. He lit a cigarette from his new black-and-silver case a little self-consciously. He watched the effect out of the corner of his eye.

Guy had ordered a bowl of ice cubes and was pretending to cool his face and hands at them, like a fire in reverse. The waiter who brought their drinks looked bored. It struck Max how foolish they must think their customers. They had seen it all; they remained unimpressed. What must it be like, to be a waiter?

'Your mother wasn't expecting us, was she?'

'No, no. Not in the slightest. Well, I do sometimes drop in on her at this time of day. But it isn't expected. Just once a week usually. On a Tuesday.

'But it is Tuesday!'

'Is it? Ah well. She won't worry. She'll look at the weather, and she'll think of me, and she'll say to Davies, *'No cucumber sandwiches today, Davies. Master Guy is drinking hock-and- seltzer with his friend Maximilian, that nice boy from the country who is such a good influence,'* and – I declare! It's my turfy fellow!'

Max looked round, following Guy's stare. A

gentleman had entered and was glancing round for a table. Guy sprang up impetuously and dashed over; Max groaned inwardly as he watched him flash his most charming smile, and indicate the way to their table. The man gave an answering smile in which Max detected some amusement, and approached their quiet corner. Max rose.

'Look who's come to sit with us Maxy!' Guy's face was alight with naughtiness, and a flush bloomed on his cheek. 'Max, Max, I must present you. Oh, I'm sorry, I haven't introduced *myself* yet - and I don't know your name either - in fact, I can't do the honours at all! This is most irregular. What on earth shall we do?'

The gentleman laughed pleasantly. 'I suggest we overleap convention. My name is Dr John Watson, and I am charmed by your invitation to join you both. My thanks to you – the thanks of a thirsty man on a thirsty day.'

Max smiled. He like the man immediately. He liked his wavy hair and the crinkles at the side of his frank blue eyes and the gentle voice which held the hint of a laugh. He is in his late thirties, decided Max as they shook hands.

'Max Fareham. Pleased to meet you, sir.'

'And *I* am Guy Clements,' interjected Guy; 'And we have met before!'

They all sat down, and Dr Watson gave his order to the waiter. 'So you mentioned, Mr Clements,' he said, 'but I cannot recall the meeting, I'm sorry to say.'

'Ah, but *I* can. It was at the races, and you gave me

a lot of excellent advice, which I ignored assiduously. I lost an enormous, princely sum.'

'Ah!' Dr Watson's eyes lit up and the pleasant crinkles became more pronounced as he smiled. 'The young man with a taste for champagne! Of course. I hope you don't mind my mentioning that,' he added, glancing at Max.

'Ooh la la! Of course not!' cried Guy delightedly.

Dr Watson chuckled. 'As a medical man,' he said in his warm, friendly voice, 'I recommend champagne as a universal pick-me-up.'

'In that case,' commented Max drily, 'Guy here is in the very pink and bloom of health.'

'And so I am!' said Guy severely.

'And so I trust you *both* are, and will long remain,' said Dr Watson, raising his glass.

They look so young, thought Watson; and so happy. His heart went out to them, sitting in their new summer suits in the high-ceilinged room, looking slender and fresh and rather awkward. He wished Holmes had come with him. Good-humoured, outgoing youth might help him. He thought of his friend's rooms, and the darkling figure lying on the couch, fretting against enforced idleness or weaving his drug-induced dreams. Sunlight; he wished he could take Holmes some sunlight. He sighed, and put down his glass, suddenly aware that Max was talking about the delights of the seaside in summer.

'At least one always enjoys a breeze there ...'

'Oh indeed,' agreed Dr Watson. 'My wife is at the seaside now. So pleasant for her.'

'I suppose your practice keeps you in town?' asked Max. He could not disguise the flat note that crept into his voice at the mention of a wife.

'Yes, my practice – well, it's not a very demanding practice at the best of times,' said the doctor with a conspiratorial wink. 'And I have a friend who sometimes needs me.'

Guy stopped playing with the melting ice cubes, and Max hastily offered the Doctor a cigarette. Was this wife at the seaside sophisticated and understanding, he wondered, or just ignorant and rather dense?

'Thank you Mr Fareham,' said Watson, accepting. 'Also, I have work to clear which must be completed shortly, as I'm bound by contract.'

'How tedious for you,' murmured Guy.

'Medical work by contract, sir?' asked Max politely; 'I didn't know that was the custom – is it so many patients per month, or something?'

Dr Watson laughed heartily. 'Dear me, no! What an interesting proposition – a sort of piece work, you mean? A bushel of measles equals a week's rent? No, I'm afraid it's nothing so lucrative. I write a little.'

'Really?' asked Max.

'For the Lancet!' said Guy, putting his forefingers to his temples and speaking in a mediumistic monotone. 'I see a medical magazine. I see an article on - let's see now - on bunions ...'

'Shut up, Guy!' said Max, resting his chin on his hand and sighing. 'Is he right?' he asked their companion.

'Not exactly. It's a little less highbrow than that. For magazines, certainly – *Lippincott's*, *The Strand*, even *Beeton's*.'

'How interesting! Do you make up the stories out of your own head?'

'Not at all.' Dr Watson looked rather rueful, as though he regretted mentioning the subject. 'I may fudge the issues, but the cases are true enough.'

'Dr Watson!' exclaimed Max suddenly. 'Oh, good Lord! Of course! The weather must have hard-boiled my brain. Good grief, sir, I can't tell you how honoured I am to make your acquaintance!' He leapt to his feet, and pumped the amused Doctor's hand for a second time.

Guy looked from one to the other, agog. 'What am I missing here?'

Max's face was flushed, and his eyes shone with excitement. 'Guy, this is *the* Dr Watson – the friend of – of Mr Holmes. *You* know.' He nodded quickly at his friend, half embarrassed.

'Oh, good Lord!' echoed Guy, his voice rising up the scale. 'You mean the one you're madly – the one you admire so much? My dear sir,' he said turning to the Doctor, 'You're hardly likely to escape with your life in tact now. There is but one thing in the world that Max Fareham lives for, and that is the chance to kiss the ground that Mr Sherlock Holmes walks on.'

Dr Watson laughed. 'Oh dear!' he said.

'Shall we have another drink? Please, Doctor, you can't possibly go now!' Max ordered more drinks, eagerness overcoming his natural shyness. 'Do you know,' he said, 'I've read everything you've ever written about Mr Holmes. Tell me, is he – is he like you say he is?'

'How do you mean?' asked Dr Watson, his blue eyes twinkling.

'A – a genius. I supposed that's what I mean.'

'Well, yes. I can confirm *that* opinion. I've never written less than my true evaluation of my friend's genius. He is extraordinary.'

Max nodded encouragingly.

'But what's he like when he's *not* being a genius?' asked Guy rather insolently. 'Does he go out? Mother could invite you both to dinner, and then Maxy could swoon at his feet.'

'Be quiet!' hissed Max.

Dr Watson chuckled. 'What a kind offer. But I'm afraid he rarely dines out, and never goes into company if he can help it.'

'Ah, a recluse. How tedious he must find all this adulation,' said Guy, shaking his head sympathetically. 'But doesn't he get bored, in between cases?'

'H'mmm. Yes. I'm afraid he does.'

Dr Watson then deftly changed the subject. Max tried his best to steer it back to Sherlock Holmes, but the Doctor firmly resisted all attempts to probe.

'I must be going,' he said after a while, pulling out his watch.

'Oh, we'll walk along together,' said Guy sweetly, smiling significantly at Max.

'Well ... ' Dr Watson eyed them for a moment and then smiled. 'If you like,' he said.

The worst of the heat was over for the day, and the town was exhaling a long sigh of warm air from every brick and paving stone. They walked back through the park, Max and Dr Watson chatting pleasantly while Guy listened. After a while he began to hang back, pouting just a little; it seemed to him that Max was a touch too smitten with *his* turfy gentleman. This man's clever friend lent the doctor a halo of romance, and Max was fawning like a puppy; quite disgusting, really. He swished at a flower with his cane.

Max was walking on air. He was aware that he was saying the most foolish, boyish things, that his hair was damp and dishevelled, that his cheeks were flushed. He was conscious of Guy's disapproval. But he did not care. Dr Waston was talking with him, as an equal - as an equal! - about Afghanistan and the Battle of Maiwand. He was enthralled. And they were all three walking back to Baker Street! Would he invite them in for tea, perhaps? He hoped, he hoped that he would ...

Dr Watson was pleasantly relaxed. This outing had done him the world of good. He now felt able to tackle his next story – perhaps even make a start tonight, with a whisky and soda at his elbow. Maybe Holmes would have a case, or have cheered himself up a little. Perhaps he could even suggest dining out ... These boys were like a tonic. The young had such enthusiasm, such good humour. Charming. They were quite charming.

They reached the door of number 221B, and Watson paused. 'Well goodbye, my dear young sirs. It has been delightful to meet you.'

'Oh, yes,' said Max flatly. He had convinced himself that the Doctor would say, *'Won't you come in for tea and meet Mr Holmes?'* It must have shown on his face, for Dr Watson was saying gently, 'I'm afraid I can't invite you up. These aren't my rooms any longer, you see, and Holmes might have a client. In any case -' he wrinkled his nose - 'the place is in no fit state for visitors.'

Max fumbled inside his jacket. 'Here's my card, Dr Watson. Please do call on me if ever you're in Sussex.'

'And here's mine!' Guy handed over his own card with alacrity. 'Max is with me for a month, so there's no need to go to Sussex. Please visit – we're almost neighbours.'

Dr Watson was about to return the compliment with *his* card, when the door of 221B opened behind him, and he turned.

'Oh hello Holmes,' he said casually. 'I was just about to come up. Going out?'

Sherlock Holmes looked somewhat surprised to see so many people on his doorstep. As he descended to the street his keen gaze took in Watson's two young acquaintances, and he bowed slightly.

'Scotland Yard have summoned me, my dear – a new case, you see. At last.'

Watson noted that his eyes were bright, his

expression focussed and alert. He was dressed in immaculate black; he had not dressed properly for nearly a week, nor set foot outside the house.

'Excellent!' he said heartily, and Holmes nodded, laying his long white hand on Watson's shoulder.

'I must get on, then. Don't wait up.' He stepped past the two young men with another vague nod, and whistled for a hansom which materialised immediately.

They all looked after the departing cab. Dr Watson's astute medical eye took in Max's sudden pallor, and he decided than an invitation to tea was after all something of a necessity.

'Well, well,' he said, 'He's obviously not got a client in now, so we can go up. I would be delighted to offer you the hospitality of my old lodgings for half an hour or so.' He ushered them inside and led the way up the well-trodden stairs to Holmes' door.

'Come in, come in!' he said, adding 'Please forgive the mess.'

The room looked, if anything, slightly worse than when Watson had left it. For one thing, most of the litter from the mantelpiece had been swept onto the hearth. Guiltily, he retrieved the small Morocco case from his pocket and slipped it back in its accustomed corner. He rang the bell for Mrs Hudson, and motioned the young men to sit down.

'Excuse me a moment,' he said as he bent to scoop up some of the debris. He quickly seized the newspapers from the floor and heaped them under a cabinet – a space already partly filled by a jumble of books and papers.

Max and Guy watched, fascinated. They had cleared spaces for themselves on the couch, and Max was gingerly holding fragile piece of chemical apparatus.

'Oh, here, let me relieve you of that.' Dr Watson placed it hastily on a small, acid-stained table in the corner. 'Chemistry,' he said with a wry smile.

The Stradivarius was sitting disconsolately in the corner of Holmes' armchair. Max looked at it. 'Er, music!' explained Dr Watson unnecessarily.

Guy's eyes were riveted by a curly-toed, garish slipper balanced on the side of the coal-scuttle. 'Tobacco,' said Watson, following his gaze; he indicated the coal scuttle. 'Cigars.'

Guy slid his eyes round to meet Max's. He raised one eyebrow a fraction. Max looked up. There was an ornate monogram picked out on the wall in what looked suspiciously like bullet-holes. Dr Watson glanced up at it. He sighed. 'Revolver practice.'

He did not bother to account for the jackknife, and ignored Guy's obvious interest in the bottle on the mantelpiece, having no wish to suggest new vices to the young.

Mrs Hudson put her fiery head round the door.

'Oh, tea please, Mrs Hudson. And perhaps some of your delicious scones?' There was a distinctly placatory tone to his voice as he addressed her. Her majestic eyes swept the room, and her lips compressed to a thin, scarlet line.

'Very good, Dr Watson,' she said grimly, and

departed.

Guy looked vaguely shocked. He ran his fingers through his hair.

'Good heavens, Doctor, I hope you don't mind my mentioning it, but if I were Mr Sherlock Holmes I think I'd get myself a new maid!'

Watson suppressed a smile. 'Er, she's the landlady, Mr Clements. She owns the house.'

'Ah.' Guy was silent, digesting the information. 'Mr Holmes doesn't keep a servant, then?'

'No, no. Only occasionally a boy to run errands.' Dr Watson smiled pleasantly. 'Do you know, Holmes and I only met because a friend suggested we share the rent on these rooms?' He chuckled. 'A fortuitous chance indeed!'

Guy looked around doubtfully, noting the well-used furniture, the faded, smoke-blurred wallpaper. He said nothing. He was unable to imagine a state in which such rooms would be considered attractive enough to pay rent for. Clearly his turfy gentleman was less of a catch than he'd allowed himself to believe. He cleared his throat and looked doubtfully at Max.

Max still looked dazed. He had not yet got over his fleeting glimpse of Sherlock Holmes, and now to be sitting in Mr Holmes' own rooms verged on the frightening. He gripped the arm of the couch, and moistened his lips. Dr Watson noted his incapacity, and decided to help him to a dash of Holmes' brandy and then see them both on their way as quickly as possible.

'I think the heat has been a little trying for you both,' he said smoothly, pouring a little of the liquid into a couple of glasses. 'Here. Brandy is an excellent restorative.'

He watched Max drink, and was pleased to see the unfocussed expression he associated with shock gradually clear. Mrs Hudson's tea and scones proved to be the most effective part of the cure, however; the two young men wolfed them down, much to Watson's amusement. Holmes might have drunk half a cup of tea, buttered a scone and then left it forgotten on his plate. He mentioned this to his guests, whereupon Max began to pick languidly at his fourth scone, leaving half untouched.

Oh dear, thought Watson. I must get them away now. If Holmes comes back before they leave, I shall have a case of swooning on my hands.

'Well,' he said gently, 'I'm very much afraid I must get on with some work. It really has been most delightful. I'm so glad you were able to stay for tea.' They took the hint and sprang to their feet like startled fawns.

'Thank you, my dear sir,' said Guy with a show of urbane sophistication. 'Please do call on us. We'd be utterly thrilled to see you. And your friend, of course,' he added, 'If he cares to accompany you. We'd be charmed to meet him properly.'

Max stammered his thanks, and cast one last long look at the chaotic room.

'Yes. Please do come, Dr Watson. And should – you know, if he wanted to – then it would be – really, it would -' He backed out of the room.

Sweet boys, thought Watson. He watched them walk off down the street and disappear back into the park, talking and gesticulating wildly.

Madeleine paused. She stood silently in the doorway, checking the street. Nothing that way. Two gents that way. Good. She adjusted her hat and squared her shoulders, stepping into the street, holding the cane lightly and easily so that it sawed smoothly between thumb and forefinger as she walked. She always felt fortified by the change of clothing. It was like wearing a mask in reverse - her face was visible, but every fact about herself was hidden. The shoes were the wrong size; she had to pad them. Her heels would be blistered before the night was done.

It was a fair walk to the house, but she kept to a leisurely pace so as to draw as little notice as possible. There it was, third in the terrace. No lights showing. She walked firmly up to the door, and rang the bell: two short rings; a pause; one long ring. She waited calmly, watching the road. She felt rather than heard the door open behind her.

'Pierrot!' said the voice she expected. She turned.

'Hello Mister Louis.' Her voice was a few tones deeper than usual; a youth's voice, the accent perhaps that of a rising clerk or apprentice, the clothes with pretensions of respectability. She slipped into the house.

'Little Peterkin, how are you?' Mister Louis' voice was thick, more heavily accented than usual. He smelled of brandy.

'Not expecting me, were you?' said Madeleine.

'Mais non! To what do I owe this so great pleasure?' Louis led the way to the sitting room. It was dimly lit and warm, at the back of the house. He seated himself in his armchair, waving for Madeleine to sit opposite.

'You have information for me, Peterkin?'

'No Mister Louis. I was just calling to find out how my little present was received.' Madeleine looked confident, but very young; a lad of about fifteen, with worldly wisdom beyond his years. Louis burst into an avuncular laugh.

'I am touched, truly, by your concern for my business affairs. But you will appreciate the need for discretion.' He gazed with amused eyes at his guest, stroking his moustache.

'If I were to tell you, Mister Louis, that I might be in a position to present you with a business proposition, maybe you'd pay me a little more -'

'Money? Pierrot! That is unprofessional!'

'Respect, Mister Louis, was the word I was about to use.'

'Ah indeed. But I do respect you! You - you force me to have the respect for you. So young, and such a cynic.'

Madeleine gave a short, contemptuous sigh. 'If I were to tell you that we might be able to supply you with further instalments of the same kind of document - what would you say?'

Louis inspected the end of his cigar. 'I would say - that you are a very enterprising young man. You *and* your friends.' There was a pause. 'And I would say that there'd be no harm in my glancing over such matters, if only to advise you of their value. Or lack of it.'

Madeleine maintained an impassive stare. 'Mister Louis,' she said calmly, 'I could name at least three other parties who'd be interested.'

Louis raised one eyebrow. His mouth twitched.

'Cool. Very cool. *Tu as le sang froid.*'

'I know that that means, Mister Louis. And I have. Like ice.'

Louis nodded slowly. 'I think,' he said, 'that you are in a unique position, my Peterkin, and that I would be foolish not to appreciate your talents. Youth must be encouraged, *n'est-ce pas?* Here.' He reached into his jacket, and threw some coins onto the table. 'Bring them. What's the harm?'

'Thank you, Mister Louis.'

Madeleine had scooped up the coins and was out of the room before Louis could rise from his chair. She heard him say something indistinct as she left. She did not turn back to ask what it was.

Lady Esher absently poured tea for her guests. A shaft of morning sunlight caught her hand, modelled its plains and dimples and came to rest flatly on the white cloth. The fine china rang as she handed a cup to Max with a smile. So typical of Guy, she thought, to turn up on her morning *'At Home'* instead of the Tuesday hour she reserved for him; but at least it varied the company.

Lady Lillingford and her daughter Alicia were quite animated for once. The conversation had achieved new heights. Alicia had twice opened her mouth to speak, and on the second occasion some actual words had been emitted. What the import of these might have been, had not her mother at that moment fired a descriptive broadside of Mrs Carnforth's weekend party, Lady Esher pondered with mild interest.

Max, the dear boy, was being attentive; he was charming Lady Lillingford simply by watching her face with his deep brown eyes as she spoke. Whatever one said, if Max listened, one felt that he was giving it a flattering degree of attention.

Guy, on the other hand, was picking cherries out the madeira cake and feeding them to Candace, her pug. Candace would shortly be sick, probably in the hall by the hat stand. Really, that boy was impossible...

Lady Esher smiled dutifully at Guy, at Candace, at

the teapot and then at Max and Lady Lillingford. Alicia, she decided, needed an extra squeeze of a smile, for she looked equally fascinated and dismayed by the presence of so many young men – her eyes signified that they might number several hundred in their mild grey alarm.

'Come over here, my dear,' she said kindly. Max looked up surprised, but immediately perceived his mistake and returned his gaze to Lady Lillingford's doughy face with a hint of resignation. Alicia rose, dropped her parasol, blushed scarlet, and dutifully navigated her way around the tea table to sit beside her hostess.

'Now *tell* me,' Max heard Lady Esher say with an air of delicious confidentiality, 'Tell me about all your conquests at the party!' Alicia's response was inaudible. Max felt very sorry for her.

'And *then*, my dear, who do you think was announced?' breathed Lady Lillingford, and he patiently returned to his contemplations. Composed and serious as his face was, his mind was quite elsewhere; not one word of her long account had registered in his understanding. As he watched the loose, pale lips forming and ejecting their words, his mind moved in realms of gold and pearl, reviewing and re-inspecting the austere, possessed figure emerging from the dim hallway of 221B Baker Street. In his heart was ineffable bliss, exquisite pain. He sighed unconsciously as Lady Lillingford concluded her description of the Duchess of Devonshire's ball gown.

This young man has taste, she noted with approval; taste, good manners, and obvious breeding. But does he have prospects? If so, Alicia could do worse ... she changed the subject abruptly, barely pausing for breath as she set about the task of exploring Max's background with the all subtlety of an Amazonian explorer wielding a machete.

Guy had discovered that there was a limit to the number of cherries a small, fat dog could consume. This limit had just been reached, and Candace did the decent thing and exited the room. Guy watched her go. What should he do next? His eye lighted upon Max, bravely holding his station whilst buffeted by the sou'wester of La Lillingford's interrogation. I shall rescue him, thought Guy lovingly.

'Oh, Mother!' he cried, suddenly and loudly, causing all heads to turn towards him – not because more than one person in the room was under the impression that she was his mother, but because he had hitherto spoken only four words: '*Hello,*' '*Charmed,*' and '*How tedious*'.

Guy simpered, pleased with himself. 'We met the most *fascinating* gentleman yesterday. Actually we met *two* fascinating gentlemen. The first one - he is so sweet - I'd already made his acquaintance at the races over champagne, and we were sitting yesterday in the bar at -'

'Guy, dear, please pick up that cherry before you grind it beneath your boot heel!'

Lady Esher's voice carried a warning note. Alicia's eyes had become very round; mention of 'champagne' and 'races' had quickened her breath. Lady Esher was all too aware that her son's friends - always excepting Max - were inclined to be somewhat disreputable.

'... smoking and chatting,' continued Guy, tossing the cherry onto the table, 'When there he was. And do you know what? He turned out to be a close friend - indeed, *the* close and intimate friend, of -'

'I do *hope*, Guy, that you have not issued these gentlemen with one of your invitations to dine here,' interrupted Lady Esher again, hoping to stave off the name of the intimate friend. Could it be that Beardy, or Beardsley, or whatever he called himself? Surely not that awful Wilde man ...

Lady Lillingford, on the other hand, was listening attentively. Beardies and Wildies were beyond her ken; a more illustrious Beard was in *her* mind, a Beard definitely associated with horseflesh and champagne ...

'Of course not, mother! He never dines out, you know. He is so fascinating! So *different*. And we had tea in his rooms afterwards, but he couldn't join us himself as he'd just been summoned to Scotland Yard.'

There was a small flurry as Lady Esher pressed several different kind of cake upon Alicia.

'Scotland Yard?' repeated Lady Lillingford, with a dawning realisation that the P of W was not, after all, the protagonist of this adventure.

'Yes, Lady Lillingford!' emphasised Guy gaily, aware that he was making an impression. 'He is professionally associated with Scotland Yard - you must know that.'

'*Who* is, dear?' Lady Esher felt she could begin to relax. Sir Edward Carson, could it be?

'Mr Sherlock Holmes, of course! I *told* you!'

'No dear, you never mentioned the name.'

'Only because you kept interrupting me, going on about cherries and dinners and suchlike.'

'Mr Sherlock Holmes?' repeated Lady Lillingford slowly; 'Ah, yes! My dear, it's that wonderful detective man - you know, he cleared up the matter of Lord St Simon's little problem so discreetly. *You* remember, dear. Mrs Tattershall told us about it a while ago. Shocking business.'

Lady Esher metaphorically unstopped Alicia's ears by withdrawing the tray of cakes, and seemed remarkably to have unstopped her mouth in the process.

'But I have read all about him, Mr Clements! He is remarkable, as you say. It must have been wonderful to meet him in the flesh.'

Her small, clear voice turned all heads in her direction, and Max nodded vigorously, his heart swelling with affection for Alicia. Guy had more than appropriated his hero in the last few minutes, and he was determined to retrieve the honour.

'We didn't really have time to introduce ourselves, Miss Lillingford; he passed us on the doorstep.' Max blushed deeply. 'But we had tea with Dr Watson in his rooms.'

'And what rooms!' crowed Guy; 'Utterly *Bohemian*, Miss Lillingford! So thrillingly unconventional!'

'Bohemian?' Alicia leaned forward, fascinated; Lady Esher thought she detected an unhealthy gleam in her eye.

'Yes, yes! Oh, how can one describe them? Filled with chaos, but such *artistic* chaos! Chemistry, tobacco, Persian slippers. Revolver practice. You see, he eschews all the petty concerns of daily life and lives in splendid isolation, either driven by the white heat of his genius, or - or -'

Max chose not to leap into the breach and save his friend; really, this was too much. Guy knew nothing whatever about Mr Holmes.

'Well, well,' said Lady Esher mildly into the the pause that followed, 'Obviously a remarkable man. Perhaps we *could* invite him to dine one evening – with Mr Percy, Sir Edward's solicitor, and other people of that sort.' She smiled wearily at Lady Lillingford. 'One does well to entertain one's professional men from time to time, don't you find? They do give of their best when favoured with good wine and conversation.'

Lady Lillingford nodded. 'Oh, quite – Sir Charles' physician is a charming man, quite convivial company in the right circumstances.'

Max could not bear it. 'He would not come, Lady Esher, I think,' he said in stilted tones, straining the boundaries of politeness. 'As Guy has already mentioned, he does not dine in company.'

Both ladies looked taken aback, and his hostess raised a well-bred eyebrow. There was an awkward hiatus before the conversation picked up harmlessly again, and Guy sulkily began to pick walnuts out of the walnut cake. The shaft of sunlight pressed itself into the nap of the carpet, and slept at its twisted roots.

The breakfast table at 221B Baker Street was also bathed in warm yellow. The blind was up, the windows were open and the noise of mid-morning traffic chattered behind the ticking of a clock and the occasional crackle as Sherlock Holmes turned the pages of his newspaper. Dr Watson was relaxing in the warm sun, smoke curling from his cigarette.

'Watson.'

'H'mmm?'

'Who were those two young men you entertained for tea in my rooms yesterday?' Holmes spoke from behind his newspaper.

'Oh - just an acquaintance, and the friend of an acquaintance. I met them when I went out for a walk.'

'Obviously.'

'Admirers of yours, as it happens.' Watson pushed a crust of toast around his plate and smiled at the shimmer of sun on the silver coffee pot.

'I would have thought admirers of *yours* would be a more apt description. Your little stories are gaining you a reputation you know, however inaccurate they may be, and however inappropriate a form in which to embody my professional achievements.'

'You never read them, Holmes, so I don't see how you can judge.' Watson smiled again, and poured the remains of the coffee into his friend's cup.

'I've glanced at one or two,' sighed Holmes, laying

aside the paper and taking up his pipe. 'It seems to me that you take some quite unjustifiable liberties, not only with the material but also with my character.'

'So you keep saying, my dear. You haven't finished your coffee.'

Holmes picked up the cup absently, and sipped.

'You look better today,' ventured his friend; 'Might I enquire about investigation on which you're currently engaged?'

'You might, my dear fellow, but I'm not yet able to give you much information. It's a Government matter.' Holmes passed a thin hand over his hair. 'Brother Mycroft is responsible for involving me. Some War Offices documents have gone missing; of no great moment in themselves I understand, but related to the nation's security nonetheless.'

'You were away all night?' asked Watson carefully.

'Indeed. But so far I have little to go on. Perhaps you'd care to join me today in a number of enquiries I'm planning? That is, if you've nothing planned yourself – meeting your young drinking companions again, for instance?'

Watson ignored the sarcasm and met the grey eyes innocently. He was delighted to see a return there of the usual sparkle.

'I was not planning anything of the kind today; I may stroll over tomorrow and return their call,' he said lightly.

Holmes rose from the table and wandered towards the mantelpiece. His silk dressing gown was knotted carelessly at the waist, but his appearance was otherwise as fastidious as ever. Watson marvelled anew that one so untidy, indeed so wilfully destructive, in his personal habits should be so neat, so correct in his dress.

'You're invited too, by the way,' he added.

'Oh?' Holmes was inspecting his violin, plucking gently at the strings and listening minutely to their resonance. After a moment, he murmured, 'I never call on anyone. You know that, Watson.'

'Only if it's after midnight,' said Watson *sotto voce*. 'You should, you know,' he added in a louder voice. 'It would do you good.'

'If I call on you after midnight, Watson, it is because I am in need of your help. And I do not require good to be done to me. Thank you.'

He drew the bow across the instrument, paused to make an adjustment, and began to play; an eerie, wandering improvisation, ill-adapted to the sunny day outside.

Madeleine worked slowly. She polished the dining-room grate methodically, rubbing the brass fender which reflected the ends of her fingers in a distorted curve. Sarah sensed her absorption, and put it down to one of two causes: love or money. Knowing Mary, she thought, it was unlikely to be love. She was a deep one, was Mary; never told you what was going on in that head of hers. No harm in asking, though, was there?

Madeleine parried her questions, and finally her jibes, with the same impassive silence. Her young face was an impenetrable mask.

Mike had spoken to her last night. They'd conversed in whispers at the kitchen table, the stump of a candle burning between them.

'This is a big thing, Mads. The biggest yet.'

'I thought that too. Mister Louis was interested, all right. The old bastard - he'd work a fast one if he could.'

Michael snorted. 'Naturally. Wouldn't you?'

'There's more to him than meets the eye, Mikey. I had him down as a high-class dealer with a nice little sideline in blackmail, but now I'm not so sure. Those papers were definitely something special.'

'Say that again. My gent had the shakes. Couldn't even get it up.' Michael laughed harshly; Madeleine did not smile. 'Sorry Mads. Humour of the trade. But he had other things on his mind once I'd put our little proposition to him.'

'Will he deliver?'

'Oh, he'll do anything. Cleveland Street's put the wind up all of them.'

'H'mmm.' Madeleine pinched the warm tallow into four sharp corners. 'Mister Louis is onto something big, and I mean to get us our proper portion. Pity we can't pull him, too.' She looked at her brother. '*Could* you pull him, Mikey?'

'How should I know? You're the one who sees him. Is he mandrake?'

She shrugged. 'Don't hang around to see.'

'You'd know by now, Mads.'

'Yes. I would.'

They were silent for a minute, Michael rubbing his eyes. They were red-rimmed, and his face was tired and white. 'I need my beauty sleep,' he yawned.

Madeleine sat looking into the candle flame. 'He's like a blank page, he is. You can't read him. He's a gent, though, for sure.'

'So, he's a gent, so what? What do we care, gent or Jew, so long as he pushes the sovereigns our way?' Michael waved a hand in the air dismissively. 'He's a spy, is what *I* think.'

Madeleine looked up sharply. 'That's what I think too,' she said calmly.

'Well it's no concern of ours, Mads. What do we care?'

'It makes it - bigger, that's all.'

'Bigger the risk, bigger the money. This could be it, Mads – our way out. This could change our lives.'

'Yes. It could.' Madeleine nodded in agreement, clenching her small white teeth.

Her attention gradually focussed on her work again. She was polishing smooth mahogany now, running the cloth over the satin surface. Rough red hands, smooth satin wood. Mike's hands are as smooth as this wood, she thought lovingly. He's a good boy. He cares about us, and he's brave. A flicker of affection warmed her cold blue eyes. *I'm brave too*: the thought half formed, and was absorbed into the rich glow of the mahogany.

She was startled by a shout of laughter from the drawing room; the gents were back. She gathered her things and hastened to follow Sarah out of the room. Lingering briefly in the hallway she saw Mr Clements through the open door, sitting on the edge of the table while his friend picked out a tune on the piano. His hair was caught in a flame of sunlight, his face smooth and golden as a girl's. He looks like Mikey would look, thought Madeleine.

As she watched, he turned his head, a delighted smile dying on his lips when he saw her. Hurriedly she turned away and scuttled towards the back stairs, one resentful thought echoing in her mind: he looks like Mikey *should* look.

'Maxy, Maxy my cherub,' cooed Guy, 'You were an *angel* to be so sweet to Mother. She was so impressed with you that she's actually given me a teeny-weeny little advance with which to show you the delights of London! I didn't even have to ask for it! And you listened so patiently to the Awful Lillingford. She thought you were an angel too. She wants Alicia to be your sweet little wifey, and she wants to know how much money your father has.'

'Oh, *don't*,' groaned Max, sitting unhappily on the edge of the piano stool. 'It was awful. And what on earth were you thinking of, going on about Mr Holmes like that?'

'Oh!' cried his friend happily, 'I *was* rather good, wasn't I? Did I shock you dreadfully?'

'Yes.'

'Did I shock *them* dreadfully?'

'Not in the slightest, Guy.'

Guy let out a shout of laughter. 'Oh come! I thought a glimpse into the murky depths of Bohemia would be just a teeny bit shocking?'

Max revolved on the piano stool, coming to a halt facing the instrument. He began to pick out *Fur Elise* with one hand.

'*He* plays the violin, doesn't he?'

'Yes, what of it?'

'Do you suppose he's as devilish as Paganini?'

'Why on earth should he be devilish, Guy?'

He turned to look at his friend, who was sitting on the table in the sunshine looking suddenly annoyed.

'I shall get rid of her. I shall. The insolence!'

'Pardon?'

'That housemaid. She was standing there looking in, as bold as you please!'

'Well, the door *is* open. It's human nature.'

Guy allowed the annoyance to evaporate from his expression, but he rose and closed the door before coming to push Max half off the piano stool so he could sit beside him. They began to improvise a duet.

'No, I should think he's quite soulful when he plays,' resumed Max, trying out a simple bass under Guy's extravagant scales.

'How do you know he has a soul to be soulful *with?*' Guy crashed an ominous chord.

'Oh, come on.'

'He *looks* like a soul in torment.' Guy lent over Max to strike a deep, uncomfortable harmony.

'So you're admitting he has one.' Max stopped playing and watched his friend's slender fingers walk up the keys atonally. He pinched his ear.

'Ouch! Well, he doesn't exactly look full of the joys of life, does he?'

Max thought for a moment. 'He looked – strained. That's true.'

'And thin. And pallid.'

'Mmm. He takes cocaine.'

Guy stopped playing abruptly. 'How do you know?'

'*You'd* know, if you read Dr Watson's stories. He

makes no secret of it.'

'Does he visit opium dens, and places like that?'

'Probably. Does it matter?'

'Well,' said Guy licking his lips, 'That *is* Bohemian. I thought there was something fishy about that room.'

Max sighed. 'He's just - wonderful.'

'You really mean that, don't you?' said Guy thoughtfully, taking his hand.

'Don't *you* think he's wonderful?'

Guy pursed his lips. 'Well. He looked. Yes, I must agree that he *did* look … but Maxy, you care for *me* best, admit it!'

Max in answer put a hand behind Guy's head and kissed him for a long time.

'You do that very well,' said Guy when he could speak.

'Oh, that was just the practice run.' He looked into Guy's eyes, noting the tiny golden flecks in the iris, the bloom of white strands making up the light blue. They kissed again, seriously.

'Let's go upstairs,' said Guy.

The house was pleasantly situated, thought Dr Watson; a tall, white, flat-fronted building in a quiet but fashionable square. Highly desirable, as a house agent might say.

Watson climbed the steps and rang, turning to look back at the smooth grass and formal flower beds snugly positioned behind gleaming black railings. He felt grateful for the shortness of the walk for he was tired, having spent yesterday criss-crossing London between the War Office and the Diogenes Club with Holmes. It might not be the most intricate of investigations, but his friend was certainly clutching at it with enthusiasm. Last night he'd gone out at around ten, disguised as a foreigner for some reason; he'd looked convincingly Latinate, with darkened complexion and rakish get-up. Watson had been unable to suppress a giggle when he saw him, whereupon Holmes had berated him in excellent, rapid-fire Italian and slouched on his way. He had not come back by the time Watson retired, and had not been at breakfast this morning. He wouldn't rest now, until he'd followed the trail all the way to the quarry.

Watson had contemplated waiting in for the snippet of news that Holmes might return with, but had decided instead to take the short walk to his young friends' house and return their call. He'd left the address with Mrs Hudson, with instructions to send on any message, and experienced a guilty pleasure at the prospect of being otherwise engaged should a summons arrive.

The door opened; a smart manservant took his card and ushered him into an alarmingly furnished drawing room. Watson waited by the window, looking out at the square and humming softly.

There was a clatter on the stairs, followed by a silence at the door as of someone composing himself to enter. Then both Mr Clements and Mr Fareham came into the room, looking rather pale and betraying symptoms of a late night and overindulgence in alcohol. Watson smiled at them, feeling almost elderly by contrast.

'Oh Dr Watson! I can hardly express how pleased I am that you've come!' said Guy, holding out his hand. 'Maxy, ring for some tea.'

Max did so, and came to sit softly by the chair that Watson took at Guy's invitation.

'Yes, I have come to return your call. It was such a fine day -' he waved a hand at the sunny square - 'and I felt in need of some gentle exercise.'

'And how *are* you, sir?' asked Max, his serious brown eyes fixed on Dr Watson's face.

'I am very well, thank you. And you, Mr Fareham? Are you still enjoying your stay in town?'

'Oh, yes. Guy has been most attentive. He's been showing me all of London's advantages.'

'Not all at once, I hope,' smiled Watson.

'Oh, Max has been to most places - last night,' said Guy with a musical laugh.

'He is trying to tire me out,' said Max, 'So that I have to go back to Sussex and recover.'

'Not true!' protested Guy. 'I just don't want him to get bored, Doctor.' He pinched his friend's arm.

Max smiled, and shook his head. He hesitated before asking carefully, 'And how is your friend, Dr Watson? Mr Holmes, I mean.'

'Better,' said Watson. 'Thank you for enquiring.'

'As he been ill, then?' asked Guy in surprise.

'No, no. But unlike Mr Fareham he has been bored, which with him is almost the same thing.'

'Ah,' said Guy seriously, 'He suffers from *ennui*. So do I, Dr Watson. So many of the really interesting people do, don't you find?'

A pleasant young housemaid entered bearing a tray. She placed it unobtrusively near Guy, and he waved to her to pour tea for them.

Max spoke quickly, before his friend could expand upon the symptoms of *ennui*. 'Mr Holmes has a case?'

'Why, yes ... but of course, you were there, were you not?' Dr Watson took a cup of tea from the maid with a kindly smile. 'Yes, he has a case. Government work again.'

'Really?' said Max, taking a cup.

'Yes. Some papers have gone missing; but I'm really not at liberty to say more.'

'Quite, quite,' nodded Max.

'Thank you, er, Mary,' said Guy languidly. 'That will be all.' The girl curtsied, and withdrew.

Dr Watson chuckled. 'He's in his element at the

moment, working in disguise by night, probably in the least savoury of areas.'

'How fascinating!' said Guy; 'Where would they be, exactly?'

'I have not the least idea, Mr Clements! And even if I did, you'll appreciate that I cannot betray his area of operation.'

'Yes, yes,' agreed Max emphatically. 'Although it would, of course, go no further. But even so ...'

'But Dr Watson!' cried Guy tenaciously, 'I was not prying, I assure you. I just wondered which, in your opinion, are the least savoury areas in town?'

'Guy!' laughed Max, 'If you intend to set up a tour of them for my benefit, please understand here and now that I've had enough excitement already. The Cafe Royal and the Criterion are quite decadent enough for me!'

Watson laughed. 'Oh, the Cri! One of my old haunts.'

Happily he began to tell his young friends of his wilder days, his army career and the occasion of his return to England. Soon all three were roaring with laughter; Dr Watson was an adept storyteller, and had a repertoire of tales guaranteed to entertain. He gave a particularly amusing account of his first meeting with Holmes and his bewilderment at his new acquaintance's eccentricities that held Max spellbound; his thirst for information about his hero was insatiable.

The visit had extended beyond the customary time,

and Dr Watson was just preparing to leave when there was a ring at the doorbell.

'Who on earth can that be?' Guy frowned in annoyance as he sidled over to the window and peeped round the curtain. 'Oh, damnation, it's Mother. What on earth does she think she's doing, coming round at this hour?' He cast an appealing glance at Dr Watson. 'Really, the liberties mothers take these days!'

Watson smiled, and rose to his feet. 'It's obviously high time I was on my way, Mr Clements. It has been a most enjoyable hour.'

He shook hands with both of them, and was just about to exit the room when Lady Esher materiaised in the doorway, her face flushed and anxious, her elaborate hat askew.

'Guy, darling! Something dreadful has happened!' she cried, apparently oblivious to the presence of a stranger in the room.

'Mother, please!' protested Guy as she overpowered him with creamy lace; Dr Watson and Max stepped discreetly into the hallway.

'I will take my leave Mr Fareham,' said Watson quietly. 'I do not wish to intrude upon a family crisis.'

'No, of course not.' Max held out his hand again, and the Doctor shook it warmly.

'I've no wish to pry, Mr Fareham, but should this prove to be a matter requiring investigation I'm sure Holmes would help. He uses the utmost discretion when dealing with family issues.'

'Thank you, Dr Watson. Thank you very much. I

shall certainly mention it to Guy. Er, please convey my respects to Mr Holmes...'

Dr Watson inclined his head, and turned towards the door. The servant opened it for him, and he stepped out into the sunlight.

Max returned with a sigh to the drawing room. When he entered it he saw with surprise that Guy looked hardly less stricken than his mother.

'What on earth has happened?' he asked, looking from one ashen face to the other in alarm.

'A burglary...' whispered Guy through blanched lips.

'My diamonds! My diamond necklace!' wailed Lady Esher.

'Oh - dear,' said Max, sinking into the nearest chair.

'Mads, this is really serious.'

Michael was nervous, glancing round, scrutinising faces as they passed and drawing back into the shade when he was met by any answering curiosity.

'Bloody hell Mike, *I* know that!' hissed Madeleine. 'Look, panicking won't help, and I haven't got long. Sarah said she'd cover for half an hour. What have you heard?'

'What *haven't* I heard! My bloke - the civil servant - he delivered last night, but that's it. No more. They're onto him.'

'*Who?* Who's onto him?' Madeleine gripped her brother's arm.

'Christ, *I* don't know. The police, I suppose. Who else?'

She looked away, up the avenue of trees, biting her lip. 'Tell me everything.'

'Right. He came last night. Sweating, he was, white as a sheet. Said he couldn't get no more, there's an investigation starting. He's going to have to leave the country, today if he can. It's that serious.'

'Did he look like he'd squeal?'

'He's scared enough to, that's for sure. I had to remind him what it'd do to his wife and family.'

'And he doesn't know your name.' Madeleine said it firmly, but her eyes were scared.

'*He* doesn't. But on the circuit, they know me. I've been careful, Mads – no-one could've been carefuller

– but if they made him talk, it'd only be a matter of time.'

'Right.' Madeleine thought for a moment, biting her lips hard. 'Listen, Mikey, I heard something today. It may not be the police at all. That private detective's on to it. You know, the clever one that sprung the rattle on the Sullivan gang. His Doctor friend was round at my gent's house this morning, and he let something slip while I was serving the tea.'

Michael sucked in his cheeks. 'That's it then, Mads. We'd better jump. He's good, that one. He's the best.' He stood back from her, his eyes hollow with fear.

'All right, all right.' Madeleine spoke calmly. 'Where are the papers?'

'I've got 'em here, still on me. I haven't been home.' He'd been walking the streets since dawn, fearful and alone. Madeleine held out her hand.

'Give them here. I know where to hide them. You go off now. Don't go home, get yourself up to Caddy's place. She's kind to them in lavender.'

Michael looked undecided. Madeleine took her brother's small white hand and pressed it. It was cold and grubby, with dirt beneath the fingernails, but silken smooth.

'I can handle it, Mikey. I'll be okay. I'll hide them at my gent's house - who'd think to look there? Couldn't be better. And nobody knows me. Even Mister Louis doesn't know me. He knows Peter. And if they did get on to me, asking questions and that, what do *I* know? A respectable working girl like me - don't know what my brother gets up to in his spare time, do I? Shocked out of my mind, I'd be!'

She widened her eyes in mock horror; Michael had to smile. Deftly he drew a sheaf of papers from beneath his jacket and pressed it into his sister's hands. She clutched them to her for a moment, then quickly secreted them in the bosom of her dress.

'Caddy's then,' he said. 'Any dosh?'

'You know where.'

'Right. I'll expect to hear when all's clear.'

'You will. Take care.'

She planted a kiss on his smooth, white cheek, then turned away hurriedly and threaded her way back through the trees. Michael watched her go, her straight back and high head radiant with courage. He sighed, a long exhalation of exhaustion and relief; then after looking carefully about, moved nonchalantly out of the shadows and into the sunlight.

When Dr Watson arrived back at Baker Street, he found Holmes already in. He was curled up in the armchair, his knees drawn up and his head lolling against the wing of the backrest. He was fast asleep.

Watson crept quietly into the room, placed his hat on its old peg and decided to use the duration of his friend's nap to carry on with his account of the Openshaw case. He seated himself at the table, bit the end of his pen, and re-read what he had last written.

'Pray give us the essential facts from the commencement, and I can afterwards question you as to those details which seem to me to be most important.'

Watson shuddered. Thank goodness Holmes did not really talk like that; it would be quite insufferable. He'd really said something like, *'Please go on, Mr Openshaw. I will ask you to clarify any details afterwards.'*

He smiled lovingly at the figure curled up like a cat in the armchair. Holmes *was* very catlike, he thought. He possessed the essential feline qualities: focus, grace, stealth and single-mindedness. And a refusal to be drawn by flattery. Watson yawned. Suddenly Mr Openshaw's case seemed less than inviting. Perhaps he could take a nap too. Just a short one. A cat-nap.

He woke to the mingled smell of strong tobacco and hydrochloric acid. Opening his eyes, he saw Holmes bent over his deal-topped table, heating a vessel on the bunsen burner. He sat up and yawned. He disliked sleeping on the couch; it gave him a stiff neck.

'My dear Watson, I really think you have very little excuse for napping in the middle of the day. You slept well last night, and can hardly have walked more than a mile. Unless the company of your young friends was inexplicably tiring.' Holmes turned to look at him with a sardonic smile.

'No, they were as amusing as ever. How, may I ask, do you know where I have been?'

'Mrs Hudson showed me the address! And before you ask, she also told me that you breakfasted at the usual hour, so you obviously had no need to compensate for a broken night by lying in.'

'And *you*, I take it, got no sleep at all last night,' said Watson as he rang the bell for tea. 'At least you've washed that horrible stain off your face. You looked alarmingly foreign when last I saw you.'

Holmes' smile broadened, and he smoothed his black hair.

'The essence of disguise is the *inner* change. Ask any actor. I looked foreign because I *felt* foreign. In any case, it proved effective enough for me to have another try tonight; indeed it's imperative that I do so.'

'Indeed? And may I ask what nature of enquiries necessitate this elaborate disguise?'

'No, you may not,' retorted Holmes gleefully.

'Then you must be involved in some disreputable and sordid activity,' said Dr Watson loudly as Mrs Hudson's fiery head appeared round the door.

'Oh, tea please Mrs Hudson,' said Holmes smoothly without looking up.

'Really Watson, you're being most provoking,' he added when she had gone. 'Mrs Hudson expressed herself quite strongly to me recently on certain subjects, and I made superhuman efforts to soothe her. Please refrain form stirring her up again.'

Watson chuckled. 'What were the subjects?'

'Oh …' Holmes turned, leaning an arm over the back of his chair. 'Little matters such as damage to her property.' He indicated a large hole burnt in the rug. 'Acid.' He shrugged humorously. 'And, er, the other little matter of the plaster.' Watson followed his eyes to the various motifs emblazoned on the wall. The *'V.R.'* was merely the most obvious.

'I explained patiently and carefully that it was a matter of life and death with me to keep my hand in.'

'And what did she say?' Watson was grinning like a schoolboy.

'She raised the rent!'

They both burst out laughing, even as the good lady herself entered with a tea tray. Holmes sprang up and cleared a space on the side table.

'Oh thank you, Mrs Hudson. How lovely,' he said with a winning smile. Few could resist Holmes' charm when he chose to exercise it, and Mrs Hudson was seen to smile back at him, and Mr Holmes to wink at Dr Watson as she departed.

'Now then,' said Watson as he handed his friend a cup of tea, 'I *insist* on knowing why my closest friend is dashing about the seedy side of London in the dead of night disguised as a foreigner.'

'Oh, very well. There've been some further developments. A second set of documents has gone missing, and our suspect in the War Office was caught in the act. I say *caught in the act* as a figure of speech - Lestrade's men were so tardy in making the arrest that he had ample time to pass the papers to his contact, a young man who works the streets, and who may already have delivered them to their intended destination.'

Holmes sighed. 'We caught up with the criminal this morning, packing desperately to leave the country. It was I who tracked him down. I tell you, Watson, it was pitiful; he was acting, as I suspected he might be, under threat of blackmail. I did what I could for him. I've promised to keep his reputation as clean as possible, though he has a serious enough charge to answer in any case.'

He put down his cup and lit his pipe. He caught Watson's gaze, and a long and meaningful look passed between them.

'I told you what would happen, with the new laws. The Blackmailer's Charter. There's no question that this man would never have betrayed his country were if not for his helplessness in the other matter.'

Watson nodded seriously. There were few subjects upon which he'd heard Holmes express himself so vehemently as that of blackmail; and when it came to blackmail of this particular sort ...

'And the young man? His contact?' he asked.

'Still at large. So you see there is work to do, and urgent though it is, it must wait until nightfall.'

Holmes rose and wandered across to the window. He watched the street below for a moment, then murmured, 'Well well. I think we may be about to entertain another client. It looks like a family matter. Tedious.'

The bell rang twice in quick succession, and Mrs Hudson was heard to admit the visitors. There was a clatter of feet upon the stairs, and a murmur of voices – their landlady obviously thought it worth her while to show these clients up.

There was a cursory knock at the door before it was flung open and their visitors were announced, in ringing tones: Sir Edward and Lady Esher.

'It's no use!' wailed Guy. His face was buried in a pile of silken cushions. Max watched the dishevelled blond head compassionately.

'What did you say?' he asked gently.

'I said,' wailed Guy in a louder voice, 'I said - oh, what does it matter?'

He threw the cushions onto the floor and turned over to face the back of the couch. 'I shall be discovered and exposed to ignominy.'

Max sighed. 'If only,' he said hesitantly, 'You'd simply told your mother the truth when she first came. Everything would be so much simpler. She could have told Sir Edward she'd merely mislaid them.'

'Oh for goodness' sake, don't be so utterly reasonable and maddeningly full of hindsight. I didn't *think* in that way. It is not in my nature to calculate consequences. I see things as the artist sees them, in their heights and theirdepths.'

'Yes,' agreed Max drily.

'A burglary seemed the best explanation to cover me,' sniffed Guy.

'And now you've persuaded your mother that an audacious gang of thieves has had access to her home.'

Guy looked at Max with watery eyes.

'And in your efforts to convince her, you suggested that this access may have been pre-arranged, causing her to suspect every hard working servant in her household.'

Guy shook his head. 'Don't be silly, Max. It's not as though she's going to find anything out and dismiss anybody, is it? I was just casting around, for – for – oh, I should have bitten out my tongue rather than go to Mother's morning at home!'

Max looked a little nonplussed. 'Beg pardon?'

'It was there - oh, fatal mistake - that she first heard the name *Mr Sherlock Holmes*. From my own lips. Oh!'

Two big tears welled up and spilled from Guy's eyes. Max went to sit beside him. He stroked his hair.

'Guy. Don't be so upset. He's not the police, is he? They haven't gone to the police - that's good, isn't it?'

'Is it?' sniffed Guy.

'Of course it is. The police would be much worse - they could bring charges, and suchlike. Mr Holmes operates in private. He'll just - investigate. And he *is* open to reason. Look -' he pushed the damp hair back from Guy's forehead - 'We're friends of his friend. That counts for something, doesn't it? Dr Watson will speak for you. He'll vouch for your character.'

Guy bit his lip. Then suddenly, his whole expression brightened.

'Max! Maxy, my most beautiful, intelligent, persuasive Maximilian!'

'Thank you!' said Max.

'*You,* my darling boy, you, my beloved, will to go Mr Holmes and plead my cause. You will fix him with your doe-like gaze and say -' Guy leapt from the couch and cast himself at Max's feet, hands clasped in supplication - 'You'll say, he is a poor fatherless boy, sir, who knew no better. Led astray by me. Led astray by the Fiendish Fareham. Punish me, sir, but let Guy Clements be pardoned!'

Max pushed him over with his foot. 'Be off, you importunate young rascal, and leave me to my deductions!' he growled sternly.

'You will carry on regardless of that cruel rebuff. You will clasp his knees and kiss his hand, like this' - he kissed Max's hands passionately - 'and you will say, Oh what a falling off was there! Have pity! And he'll say, My dear young sir, your youth and beauty have moved me. I will spare Guy Clements for your sweet sake!'

'Yes, yes. Go on,' laughed Max.

'And he will raise you with his own hands, and offer you tender consolation. And, er -'

'Yes? Yes? Yes?'

'And then you'll come home to me, and I'll order a magnificent feast in your honour!'

'Oh.' Max pouted. 'I was hoping he'd require some sort of recompense. You know. For having spared you.'

'Maxy!' Guy's eyes were very wide. 'If *that's* your intention, I think I should make sure Dr Watson will be out of the way when you go.'

Max sobered suddenly. 'You're serious, aren't you?'

'*Of course* I'm serious!' yelled Guy.

'No. Oh, no.' Max shook his head very slowly and deliberately.

'But,' pleaded Guy, his eyes starting to brim again, 'Maxy, sweet darling boy, you must, you absolutely *mu*st! It's the Only Way. And you know you've been dying to meet him. Please.'

Max said nothing.

'Please! Please! Picture it: you sit there, looking your beautiful self, and he sits opposite, fixing you with those keen eyes …'

Max quailed. 'No.' He blushed. 'I can't. I'm too shy.'

'*Shy?*' bellowed Guy, '*Shy?* He is shy, if you please, when his best friend stands in danger of Pentonville. Hard luck, Guy, enjoy your time in gaol, I'm too shy. Thank you. Thank you *very much*.'

'Oh. God. Do it yourself, then.'

'I can't. Oh, I can't. Think of the shame!' Guy hid his face in his hands. 'I would never get over it. Never.' His voice broke.

'You don't seem to care much about *my* shame,' pointed out Max feelingly.

'Oh, but I do! I do, because your shame would be so much greater if you had to watch your dearest friend suffering in the dock.' Guy spoke in a muffled voice from behind his hands. 'I know it would. I know your tender heart.'

Max said nothing. He watched Guy's bowed head. After a while, he leaned forward and prised his fingers apart. Guy smiled up at him radiantly. He threw his arms round his neck and kissed him.

'Thank you! Thank you! I knew you would!'

'I said no such -' Guy kissed him again '- thing!' Guy kissed him more lingeringly. 'No.'

'Yes.' Guy deftly undid Max's tie and loosened his collar. He kissed his throat. 'Oh yes. You will. For me.' His hand slid down his shirtfront.

'You are shameless,' whispered Max.

'Of course I am. Come on. Say yes.'

'No. Yes. All right. Yes,' said Max almost inaudibly. His body simply could not resist Guy; it betrayed him every time.

'Tomorrow, then.' Guy's hands were busy. Max staggered mentally in a furnace-blast of passion.

'Yes. Alright. Tomorrow.'

Several hours later, Max was regretting a new and horrible development. Guy's spirits had revived astoundingly, and after consuming the best part of two bottles of champagne he had persuaded Max to 'come slumming', as he put it.

Slumming, it seemed, involved walking anxiously down smelly, ill-lit streets dressed in unobtrusive clothing and jumping out of one's skin every time one was approached. Max's nerves were on edge; he was a defenceless and ignorant intruder. There were plenty of dark figures milling around in the night, and no doubt much of interest to see, but Max did not feel interest. He felt only fear.

A little way back, a group of youths had passed them; Max could swear that their faces were painted. Further back still, a gentleman - unmistakeably a gentleman - had accosted a fierce, filthy boy of about twelve or thirteen. The boy and the man had disappeared together into the night. Max himself had been pushed and pulled by three women with salt-white faces and eyes like pits. They'd caressed him, ruffled his hair, tried to pull him away with them. On freeing himself from their collective embrace he'd discovered that his watch and chain were missing. He was lost in the jungle, an innocent soul wandering the wastelands of Hell; he fervently wished himself back in Sussex.

Guy was drunk. He was interested in everything and everyone, and completely reckless. He was accosted on average every hundred yards, and acknowledged each encounter with a delighted yelp; his response was so effusive that the men moved on, muffling their faces. It would have been amusing had Max felt safe and relaxed, but it seemed to go on for hours and Guy insisted on taking on more liquor at every port. Max had had no idea that the 'unsavoury areas' were so – well, unsavoury. This is where they buy and sell bodies, he thought. Bodies and souls.

At last Guy seemed to be running down. Like a clockwork toy he slowed gradually to a halt, yawning widely.

'Cab!' he said suddenly to Max. 'Need a cab. Go get a cab.'

Max sighed. Where - ah, there was the road, over there. Guy sank gracefully onto a step. 'Cab!' he kept repeating like a baby bird. Oh, hell.

'All right, Guy, stay there. No, don't lie down. Just

stay there. And don't talk to anyone, do you hear? Don't – talk – to – anyone.'

Guy nodded. He looked very much the worse for wear; very young, very grubby. He looks like a street boy, thought Max; a Mary-Ann, out on the streets all night, drunk to keep out the cold and to numb himself against what he must do for a living. Max shuddered, and hurried away.

Ten minutes later he returned just in time to see his friend bid good-night to a slim, dark figure. He waved after him, and sighed.

'Oh, Maxy!' Guy focussed with difficulty on Max's face. 'What are you doing here? 'Sno place for a country - country lad.' He hiccupped loudly. 'Beautiful man just now. Italian. I sang to him. I sang '*Che faro senza Eurydice?*' He said he knew it. It was very sad.' He sniffed loudly. Max took no notice of this drivel as he hauled his friend to his feet and walked him to the waiting cab.

When they were safely on their way, Guy returned to the subject. 'Oh, such eyes, Maximil-ilian. Like yours. Deep pools. Not brown, though. Grey. Black hair. Dark skin. Beautiful. Could've taken him home. Kept him as a pet.'

'Shut up, Guy. You could've got yourself into the most awful stew just then if I hadn't come back when I did.'

'Wouldn't ha' minded, Maxy. Woulda liked it. Nah.' He stuck out a drunken tongue. Max pursed his lips, and turned pointedly away.

They arrived back home just before three a.m. Mr Sherlock Holmes, stepping down from the back of the hansom, waited only to make certain of the address before turning on his heel and walking briskly back to Baker Street.

Louis la Rothière cleared his throat softly, and took a sip of brandy. He blinked slowly at the young man opposite, pursing his lips as he formulated a response.

'Certainly your information interests me, little Peter. I think you have acted with commendable discretion. But how, may one ask, have you gained access to this gentleman's residence?'

'Never you mind how. A contact. It's completely safe - you have my word on that, Mister Louis.'

The small, pale face was set, distant. No hint of a beard yet, thought Louis. My little spy is a child, just a child. And those respectable clothes are borrowed, the shoes too big. How resourceful they are, these scraps of flotsam from the gutter. This one is exceptional.

'But you will understand,' said Louis in liquid tones, 'that I cannot possibly pay you for what you have not given me.'

'But I've got it for you. It's safe. Something in advance, and I'll bring it.'

'But why did you not bring it tonight?' Louis' eyes were hooded.

'It wasn't possible,' said Madeleine gruffly. She'd been unable to smuggle the papers home because the gentlemen had been in the drawing room when she left; if only she'd just kept them in her dress! At least they were safe inside that vase, guarded by the vigilance of a rich household. She'd heard a whisper on the streets already - a sharp stranger, asking questions.

Louis laughed coldly. 'Well, well. You ask me to believe you. But may I say that I doubt the existence of these papers, my dear young man? And I doubt the existence of this obliging gentleman also.'

'He doesn't know, Mister Louis. That's why it's safe. He's in blissful ignorance, you might say.'

'But you have a contact in his household.'

'Yes. But he doesn't know that. So I can't call on - my contact openly.'

'I see.' Louis rose and moved to the door.

'I would like to believe you, Peter, truly; but I need a more concrete assurance than this. If you cannot provide it, well -'

He flung open the door, and bowed ironically. Madeleine swallowed. She wasn't prepared to give up, not yet; but just in case everything went wrong, she needed money now. She knew who the sharp stranger was, asking questions, and Michael had taken their mutual stash to get up to Caddy's in Yorkshire.

'Clements,' she said gruffly. 'Mr Guy Clements. Melville Square. That's all I'm saying.'

Louis searched her face. Clements. He knew the name. Peter could be bluffing, but ... He reached for his wallet.

'Five pounds, Pierrot, for being a good boy.'

Madeleine took the money. 'That's five percent of what you owe me, Mister Louis.'

'Very well.' She caught a twinkle in his eye as he turned away.

'Goodbye Peterkin,' he said softly.

'Well, I find it extremely difficult to credit,' protested Dr Watson.

'Are you doubting my inferences, Watson?' Holmes' voice was sharp, though his eyes remained hooded.

'Well, no, Holmes. I know you too well for that,' said the Doctor uncomfortably. 'But you know how deceptive appearances can be on occasion. Doesn't character count for anything?'

'Character!' Holmes raised his eyes to the ceiling. 'I cannot say that the young man has any character to speak of!'

'My dear Holmes,' protested Watson, 'You're being unjust. You forget that I've met and spoken with him on three occasions, and each time the impression I received was one of youthful high spirits. Nothing more.'

Holmes appeared to be struck by the comment. He puffed on his pipe for a moment, looking narrowly at Watson.

'Well well,' he said, 'If youthful high spirits are indeed the motive, they've led him far beyond the law.' He paused. 'Watson, tell me: do you honestly believe the thoughtlessness of youth would lead a respectable young man to do such things?'

'Absolutely not, Holmes!' said Watson impetuously; then added cautiously, 'Well, so far as you've sketched the facts. But you've only outlined the bare bones of the matter, so I'm not really in a position to judge how far poor Clements might be implicated.'

Holmes drew a deep breath. 'That is because you insist upon leaping in with angry denials. If you will simply sit still and listen, I'll let you have the whole picture.' He rose, and went to fetch the Persian slipper from the coal scuttle. He pinched his friend's arm as he passed.

'Don't be offended, my dear fellow. I try never to be biased. I just follow diligently where the facts lead me.'

Watson smoothed his hair and watched Holmes busy himself with the cleaning and refilling of his pipe. It was true that he was as unbiased as any human being could be. It was also true that he rarely made so drastic a charge as this without good reason. But when Watson recalled that golden face with all its youthful folly and egotism – no. There had to be some mistake.

Having refilled his pipe Holmes laid it down unlit, leaned forward in his chair, and began to speak. His expression was hidden behind steepled fingers.

'The secondary case is of no importance really, but it demonstrates an extraordinary arrogance on the part of your young friend. It seems he actually encouraged his parents to approach me over the matter of his mother's diamonds - diamonds that he himself had purloined!'

Watson could not refrain from interrupting. 'But *how* do you know he purloined them?'

Holmes sighed patiently. 'There *was no burglary,* Watson. There is not the least sign of one – no marks of forced entry, no tell-tale footprints, no attempt to force the safe. The key was in its usual place – a location known only to Lady Esher, her husband, and her son. The lady had checked her jewels less than a fortnight earlier, and found nothing amiss. There have been no new admissions to the household - the servants all have immaculate records of many years' standing, and more importantly, none of them has a motive to jeopardise their career with so obvious a theft. I questioned them all closely - you know my abilities, I think - and could uncover nothing.'

He shifted his position to sit back in the chair, frowning. 'I must confess, though, that Lady Esher's manner throughout was not altogether natural; I did wonder briefly whether she had some hand in the business herself. But it seems unlikely - the diamonds are insured only for a portion of their value, and should she have need of money it seems she has a generous allowance to draw on. The husband is liberal and doting, if somewhat pompous; his perplexity concerning the theft was more evident, if anything, than hers. But now we come to the son. By your own account, Watson, he is a gambler, and my investigations tell me that he does have debts. I believe he took the gems at his leisure, some time during the last fortnight - he has access to the house at all times - and has pawned them to raise money. And I believe his mother now suspects as much, but does not wish to alert her husband to the possibility by halting the investigation.'

'Oh Holmes,' cried Watson, 'This is nothing! Even if he has done such a thing, why, it's a family matter. He will come to his senses and return them. No doubt there will be recriminations and so forth, but nothing out of the ordinary. And you have no firm evidence against him.'

'Not as yet, but I could easily obtain it. I have spent only two or three hours on the case. As you know, my energies have been directed to a far more important matter.'

'Yes,' said Watson, 'And now you are claiming that Guy Clements is the villain of that affair also!'

Holmes looked bleakly at his friend. 'It is a somewhat sordid matter,' he said softly. 'I put it to you crudely that Clements has been assuming the character of a Mary-Ann by night in order to blackmail his peers. In the course of these activities he has obtained, through the unfortunate man of whom I told you, some Government documents which I believe he intends to sell to a foreign power.'

'Good God, Holmes!' Watson sat back, aghast. 'This is unbelievable! You are talking about treachery!'

Holmes nodded grimly. 'I'm sorry, Watson. I came across him in his persona last night. He was drunk and indiscreet, and actually propositioned me.'

Involuntarily, Watson's mouth twitched.

'I do not see that I've said anything amusing,' said Holmes severely. 'I approached him first, I should confess, in my Italian character. The fact that he was on the streets is unusual enough, and in disguise. He fits perfectly the description given to me by the man he has driven to despair and ruin. I followed them back to his house - he was with another, whom I take to be Max Fareham - by taking a quiet ride behind their hansom. There can be no doubt whatsoever as to his identity.'

'But this is appalling, Holmes! Though surely - surely as yet all circumstantial?'

'Circumstantial? Rather singular, is it not, that such a set of circumstances should coincide? I gave a detailed description of Clements to the other man in the case, and he said he would swear this was the youth who has been blackmailing him. Moreover, do you not think it odd that he should show such determination to insinuate himself into your favour, and such interest in my activities? He has already gained access to these rooms Watson! Believe me, there's a side to young Clements that is both calculating and dangerous. He has played you for a fool, my dear fellow!'

Watson sat in unhappy silence. It was useless to protest that the celebrated Mr Holmes had many admirers; none had managed to approach so close to the detective's private life. Useless again to point out that it was Max Fareham, not his friend, who had been so persistent in his attentions; Holmes would say this was all part of the plan. Watson was uncomfortably aware that Guy Clements' youth and beauty *had* worked a little magic on him ... of course he had been guarded, discreet ... but how persistent they'd both been in questioning him about Holmes' activities - even, he remembered with a lurch, to the point of asking whereabouts in the city the disguised detective would be operating!

'I still can't credit it, Holmes,' he said; but his voice was flat, and lacked conviction.

'My poor Watson. I'm so sorry.' Holmes looked keenly into his friend's eyes. 'Believe me, I will not be slow to admit it should I find myself in the wrong; for your sake, if not for your foolish friend's.'

Thank you,' said Watson bleakly, 'But don't say it for my sake, or for Clements' - say it for his poor friend, Max Fareham. *There's* an innocent for you, even if he has been hoodwinked and led astray.'

Holmes had just opened his mouth to speak when Mrs Hudson entered, bearing an envelope. She handed it to Watson: 'Messenger brought this for you, Doctor.'

'Thank you Mrs Hudson,' said Watson as he opened it. There was a pause. Holmes busied himself in lighting his pipe, and Mrs Hudson left unobtrusively.

'Well, well. You'll be interested in this I think, Holmes.' Watson's tone was both amused and shaken. 'The subject of your enquiries wants to see me at his house.'

He passed the note to Holmes, who studied it keenly and then read aloud in a clear, ironic voice:

'Dear Dr Watson,
'Would you be able to call on me some time this

afternoon, while Max is out? There is a terribly important matter I want to discuss with you. It is utterly private, I do assure you.

'Yours affectionately,
Guy Clements.'

'What extraordinary handwriting!' Holmes looked at Watson from under his brows, and the Doctor found himself blushing. 'This is a very familiar note, is it not?'

'He's a familiar kind of boy, I suppose,' said Watson gruffly. Holmes continued to regard him.

'Watson,' he said slowly, 'You have not -'

'No I most certainly have not. How can you suggest such a thing?'

Watson rose in some heat, crossed the room and seized his hat from its peg. Holmes' gimlet gaze followed him.

'Well, you'd better go then, my dear fellow,' he said mildly. 'It may be of some import to this investigation. Be discreet, however, and more importantly, be on your guard. Do not allow yourself to be manipulated, and above all, do not indicate my suspicions.'

'Of course not, Holmes. You can count on my discretion.'

Watson made hurriedly for the door. He thought he heard his friend chuckle softly as he closed it behind him.

Left alone, Holmes rambled to and fro in his sitting

room, smoking his pipe and contemplating the small bottle on the mantelpiece from time to time. It would be hours before he could take up the threads of his investigation again, and he'd now require a full report from Watson before making any further move. Hours of empty time to kill. He sat down and picked up a newspaper, turning to the agony column and trying to absorb himself in its cryptic messages without success. He flung the paper away with an oath, leapt to his feet and seized his violin. He wandered towards the window, playing an air from Gluck's *Orfeo ed Eurydice*.

Max Fareham walked swiftly up Baker Street. He was hot and rather dusty, though he'd taken immense care over his toilette. At least, he thought, Dr Watson should to be there. He swallowed at the thought that Watson might possibly be out. Perhaps if he *were* out, he could pretend that it was Dr Watson he'd called to see, and make his excuses and leave. Or perhaps Dr Watson would be in, and *he* would be out. Max felt a surge of disappointment at the prospect. Oh dear. Maybe he could simply make himself scarce and return to Guy after a suitable length of time saying they were *both* out. But he was doing this for Guy ... he thought of Guy last night, drunk and dishevelled; then of yesterday afternoon, when - but no, he really should not think of that right now.

Oh dear. Here was the house. He could not put it off any longer. He was climbing the steps, and here was the varnished black door with the brass numbers standing out upon it. Max stood, his mouth dry and his heart pumping in his throat, and closed his eyes as he reached out and pulled the bell.

Mrs Hudson answered. He recognised her, with her unnaturally red hair under its widow's cap. She did not recognise him.

'Is Mr - er, is Doctor - is Mr Sherlock Holmes in?' he croaked.

'Go straight up,' she said with hardly a glance.

Oh Lord. He was in, then. Max climbed the stairs on leaden feet. His muscles were damp string. Violin music was emanating from behind the closed door on the landing. So that was how Mr Holmes played. He stood quite still for a moment, listening; then he knocked softly.

The music stopped. An incisive voice barked *'Come!'* He turned the handle, and entered.

He looked first towards the chairs where he and Guy had sat with Dr Watson. Nobody there. He looked towards the window. No Dr Watson to be seen. Only Mr Sherlock Holmes, standing with violin in one hand and bow in the other, fixing him with eyes of a most intense and disturbing grey. He was not smiling.

'Good afternoon, Mr Fareham,' he said.

'Good afternoon Mr Holmes, we have not met before but my name is Max Fareham and - ' it was his prepared speech, and he was halfway through it before he absorbed the fact that Holmes had addressed him by name.

'Er - you know who I am?' he quavered uncertainly.

Mr Holmes indicated the basket chair. 'Pray take a seat, Mr Fareham'. He moved gracefully to the armchair and put the violin gently down on the floor beside it.

Max sat in some confusion. Mr Holmes stretched out his legs and rested his head against the back of the chair. His eyes were hooded, and his long white fingers made a steeple before him. He appeared to be waiting, looking Max over with impersonal but disconcerting intensity.

'May I ask how you knew my name, sir?' asked Max, licking his lips.

'I recognised you, Mr Fareham,' murmured Holmes; 'You are a friend of Dr Watson, are you not? And no stranger to these rooms, I believe. Please put yourself at ease.'

Max could not think of anything he was less capable of doing. He sat back a little further in the chair, and dropped his straw hat. It rolled away on its brim to rest under the couch. Max watched its slow, deliberate journey in mortification, but before he could move Holmes had leaned swiftly out of his chair and retrieved it. He handed it gravely back to Max, with a flash of amusement in his heavy-lidded eyes.

'May I ask how I can be of assistance to you, Mr Fareham?' he asked courteously after a long pause.

'Yes, yes, of course,' said Max.

'Well?' Holmes raised a dark eyebrow.

'Ah. Well, it's not me, you see Mr Holmes. It's not my problem, I mean. It's somebody else's.'

'So you are acting on behalf of a friend,' prompted Holmes.

'Yes sir, I am. A very close, very dear friend.'

Holmes nodded encouragingly.

'It's rather difficult to explain it all, actually,' said Max, coming to another halt as his eyes met that penetrating gaze. He pulled himself together with difficulty, and cleared his throat. No further words appeared.

'Er, would it help if I offered you something to calm your nerves, Mr Fareham?' said Holmes, rising from his chair. 'Permit me to pour you a brandy. My friend Dr Watson tells me it's a great restorative.' He chuckled. 'That's what he tells me, anyway.'

Max gazed at the tall, slender figure standing by the sideboard pouring a measure of brandy into a tumbler. He tried to etch that profile on his memory, the black smooth hair, the delicate hands. He took the glass, and accidentally touched those fingers. He drew his hand away as if he'd been stung, and the tumbler rolled away to rest beneath the couch.

'Oh, my God!' cried Max, hastily mopping at the rug with his handkerchief. He stretched beneath the couch to retrieve the glass. 'I'm so sorry, Mr Holmes!'

Holmes was standing with one hand at his chin, watching Max with interest. 'You seem to wish to secrete various objects beneath my couch, Mr Fareham. Please. Please leave the rug. Just leave it – it has had far worse spilled on it. There now. Sit down, compose yourself.'

He turned away to pour some more brandy. What was the young man up to? He was in the most appalling state of nerves. He had nicked himself shaving, beneath the left jaw. He was dressed in his best clothes - everything new, apart from the hat. The hat had been worn several times; the shoes too, though they'd been buffed to a shine. He seemed incapacitated by anxiety - or could it be guilt? Holmes met the appeal of Max's golden-brown eyes and looked swiftly elsewhere. Dear me.

He watched the slender brown fingers as they received the tumbler, more steadily this time. He noted the finger ends, and remarked inwardly that the young man was a pianist of some application, and that the slight deformation of the second finger of the right hand indicated much time devoted to writing. He wondered momentarily where he got his dark colouring - that skin had a coppery tint. He wished vaguely that Watson were present.

'Thank you, Mr Holmes,' said Max meekly. 'I am better now. I am so sorry.'

Holmes waved away the apology. 'Just tell me how I can help you, Mr Fareham,' he said.

Dr Watson was shown immediately into the drawing room, where Guy was sitting at the piano playing Chopin's *Raindrop Prelude* very loudly. Watson waited politely at the door until the questionable performance came crashing to an end, the last two chords suddenly rendered *pianissimo.* Guy swivelled round on the stool to look at him, his expression dramatic and sorrowful. He rose slowly to take the Doctor's hand.

'So glad, Dr Watson,' he murmured, indicating a chair. He cast himself down distractedly upon the couch.

'You are feeling unwell, Mr Clements?' asked Watson sympathetically as he seated himself.

'Oh,' murmured Guy, 'It's nothing. It's - well, how are *you,* sir?'

'I am very well, thank you.'

'So glad,' whispered Guy, his eyes now fixed some feet above Watson's head.

Dr Watson cleared his throat. 'I received your note, Mr Clements. There is some matter you wish to discuss with me?'

Guy sighed, and passed a hand across his eyes. 'Yes. I have to speak with you, Dr Watson. You're the only friend I can trust, apart from Max of course.'

Watson watched Guy's face non-committally. 'Thank you,' he said.

'You see -' Guy rose and wandered over to the

window where he positioned himself in a shaft of sunlight - 'I'm in the most awful, awful trouble.'

Watson said nothing, but raised an encouraging eyebrow.

'I have done something dreadfully wicked,' said Guy, turning his head to gaze out into the street.

'Dear me,' said the Doctor mildly.

'Yes. And I think you know what it is, Doctor. I think you will easily deduce, yes, deduce, the horrible deed of which I speak.' He turned and fixed appealing eyes on his guest. 'I have betrayed a great trust.'

Again Watson said nothing, but held fast onto the brim of his hat.

'Your friend, the inestimable Mr Holmes, is at this moment investigating the - the crime, I know. But I want *you* to know, Dr Watson, that my only motive was - oh God -' he closed his eyes briefly - 'the sordid need for money.'

Watson wished he could take notes. Holmes would consider this most interesting. But why was the young man intent on unburdening himself to Watson? He remembered Holmes' comment about the boy's 'extraordinary arrogance' - was this the egotism of an unbalanced mind?

Guy moved back to the chairs and sat down opposite his guest, leaning forward and looking into his face.

'Do you remember, sir, that sunny day at the races when we first met? Oh, innocence, whither hast thou fled?' Guy turned to address the gas bracket with this moving apostrophe, then fixed his eyes on Watson once more. 'I do not wish to cause you the least pain Doctor, but really when you gave me that tip for the three-thirty it was the first step on the downward slope for me.'

'Oh? Oh dear,' said Watson.

'Yes.' Guy nodded eagerly.

'Well, I'm sorry - very sorry indeed, Mr Clements,' was all Watson could think of to say.

'I lost heavily, you see,' continued Guy, 'I lost awfully. It was a shock - I think it overthrew my reason momentarily. I did something - well, you know what I did - and in the end, it's not even enough.'

There was a pause. 'I don't quite understand, Mr Clements.'

'I mean that the fruits of my - ill-gotten gains,' (Guy had been about to say 'labours', but that sounded a little too righteous) 'weren't even sufficient to cover the debt. And the point is,' he went on in a more businesslike tone, 'a mere hundred pounds would see me clear. I could retrieve them then, you see. Retrieve them, return them, and repent.'

Dr Watson knit his brows. He was moved by the young man's confession, but puzzled by his manner. It seemed to his experienced eye that while the boy's actions and words bespoke penitence and shame, his underlying attitude was one of histrionic enjoyment; he had not been Holmes' associate for years without learning to see a little further than most. Did the boy not realise how serious his offences were? Had he no hint of empathy for his victim, the man whose career was now ruined and whose vulnerability he had exploited in the most heartless way? It was difficult to believe, looking at Guy's peach-golden face and baby-blue eyes, that he could be so degenerate and desperate a schemer. And for a *hundred pounds*? He could not possibly be referring to the extent of his debts, it would be ridiculous, a young man in his social position. Did he really think, then, that he could buy back the papers from the person to whom he'd sold them for a mere hundred pounds? But then - Watson observed the slight, elegant figure leaning eagerly towards him from the opposite chair - perhaps he simply did not understand the value of the papers, did not understand the enormity of his actions at all.

'I sympathise, Mr Clements, I really do,' he said guardedly, 'And I think, as you say, that I know of the deed to which you refer. But you seem to underestimate the magnitude of the offence. It's a Government matter, you know. The evidence now being gathered against you is serious. A jury might well convict on what we have already; it could even - well, technically it's a capital offence.'

'*What?*' Guy's face was suddenly stricken.

'Well, perhaps not,' said Watson, alarmed at the intensity of the reaction. 'Perhaps considering the mitigating circumstances - '

'*Capital offence?*' Guy's horror was genuine and terrible. Watson hastily delved in his breast pocket for the small bottle of volatile salts he carried with him, and passed it beneath the stricken boy's nose.

'My dear Mr Clements, you must at least have considered the risks,' he protested gently; 'After all, you planned the thing in some detail.'

'Oh, God,' said Guy. 'Take that stuff away. Oh, God. No, it was all spur of the moment. Or rather - ' he buried his face in his hands - 'I *did* plan it to a certain extent. I had to. You see that, don't you? I did have to.'

Watson tried to think of something to say. 'Look here, I know the situation is grave -'

'Grave,' echoed Guy with a death knell in his voice.

'- but Mr Holmes isn't an ogre. Perhaps something can be worked out. Perhaps if you *could* retrieve them, he could find a way to return them without implicating you.' Watson paused to think, adding less hopefully, 'Well, it's a possibility. And we can hire a good lawyer.'

'Oh, God!' said Guy.

'My dear fellow,' continued Watson, 'you can't have been completely unaware of the possible consequences of your actions, can you? Truthfully?'

Guy shook his head helplessly. 'I - but I thought - I mean, I thought I'd just get them back, and put them back, and no-one would be any the wiser!'

Dr Watson rose and took a turn about the room in some agitation. A new and horrible suspicion was forming in his mind. Supposing - just supposing - that he had been right, and Holmes had been wrong, and Guy Clements had nothing to do with the blackmail case. Why then, he must think he was referring to - and that would explain - and no wonder!

Watson's face assumed an expression hardly less stricken than his host's. What had he done, what had he said? Holmes had urged discretion on him, and now - oh God. He couldn't undo his mistake by explaining the nature of the investigation, if Guy were indeed in ignorance; but equally, he couldn't just leave the boy in this state, anxious though he was to get back to Holmes. He had to make some sort of amends.

He came to a swift decision. It was the least he could do. He took out his pocket book and pen.

'Look. Here. Here is a draft on my bank for one hundred pounds. That was what you needed, you said? Well, take it. Yes -' he tried to make Guy's numb hand grasp the paper - 'Make good use of it. And don't worry. I completely take back what I said about it being a capital offence. But I must urge you, Mr Clements: unless you want to get into even deeper trouble, *stay off the streets at night.* For your own sake.'

Watson hurriedly grabbed his hat. The poor boy. The sooner he had Holmes' permission to explain things, the better. He must go straight back to Baker Street right now.

Guy stared after him with glazed eyes.

'Oh God,' he croaked hoarsely as he heard the front door close. The bank draft slipped from his nerveless fingers, and fluttered to the floor.

'It's a matter of some delicacy Mr Holmes …'

'Yes,' said Holmes with a hint of weariness. 'So you have already told me.' He noted the fleeting mortification on Max's face, and hastily softened his manner. 'Just try to give me the facts as they rise to your mind, Mr Fareham. We will sort out the details later.'

'Yes, sir. It's Guy - Mr Clements, that is, my friend, on whose behalf I am here …'

'Yes, yes,' said Holmes, closing his eyes.

'He's got himself into the most appalling mess. And it's only because he got stung at the races; he had to borrow from a moneylender, you see, and he can't afford to pay off the debt 'til the end next month.'

'So I had deduced,' murmured Holmes.

'And I'm afraid that what with all the worry, he went astray a bit.'

Holmes opened his eyes and looked coolly at Max. 'More than a bit, I'm afraid, Mr Fareham.'

'Oh,' said Max, deflated. 'You know about it already.'

Holmes said nothing.

'But really, Mr Holmes, he didn't mean any harm! He's just impulsive, and a bit foolish.'

'You are obviously convinced of that, Mr Fareham, but I must tell you that *I* am not.'

Max frowned in confusion. 'But surely, sir, it's not so very bad. It's not even as if they're the real thing;

they're just copies, fakes.'

'Does that mitigate the crime, Mr Fareham?' asked Holmes softly. (What did he mean, *'fakes'*? This was a new development ...)

Max saw the justice of the remark. 'Well, no, I suppose it doesn't make any difference whether they're valuable or not. But all the same, sir, I thought you might - I mean, you've obviously solved the case now. You know that Guy did it. And he sent me to you to - well, to beg for mercy.'

Holmes raised a sardonic eyebrow. 'He sent you? Why not come himself?'

'Oh, he's too ashamed, Mr Holmes! He is burning up with remorse. He couldn't face you.'

Max put as much appeal into his face and voice as he knew how. Observing the gestures of hand, the nuances of facial expression, Holmes was convinced of his honesty. Despite himself, he was moved by the simplicity and loyalty behind the young man's intervention. But he remained silent, watchful.

'And that's why I've come. To appeal to you on his behalf. I can tell you that he means to get them back as soon as possible, and he will give them to you, sir, to do with as you think best.'

Well, well, thought Holmes.

'You know that he has caused intense suffering by his actions?' he said.

'Oh yes. I do. But he has suffered too. If you could have seen him, you would know.'

It seemed to Max that he was making a little headway; Mr Holmes paused, and seemed to reflect.

Then he said, 'Look, Mr Fareham, I will not deny that I'm impressed by your words and by your honourable motive. But the matter has gone too far to be left. Other parties are implicated, and one at least stands in danger of a prison sentence, or worse.'

Max looked perplexed, but did not dare to interrupt.

'There are few crimes I abhor so utterly as that which Guy Clements has committed. Especially when his motive was a debt incurred through gambling, which could in any case be discharged at the end of next month. A very poor mitigation, in my view.'

'Oh, but Mr Holmes,' said Max desperately, 'Doesn't your friend Dr Watson go to the races? Surely anyone can have a run of bad luck!'

Holmes gave a wry smile. 'Dr Watson has never yet stooped to theft and blackmail, I'm happy to say.'

'*Blackmail?*' Max blanched, and gripped the arms of his chair.

'You didn't know?'

'But no! Good God! No, I don't believe it!'

Again, Holmes was convinced of the young man's truthfulness. Watson was correct, then - Max Fareham was an innocent of the first water. And yet Holmes himself had seen this same innocent in the company of Clements on the streets just the other night. He resolved to probe a little further.

'Tell me Mr Fareham, does Mr Clements often take you with him when he goes on the streets?'

'Pardon, sir?' stammered Max, completely out of

his depth.

'The streets, Mr Fareham. Those unsavoury quarters where none go save with a plain and dark purpose.'

'I'm not sure what you mean, sir,' faltered Max, 'Why should he, I mean we - oh, yes, we were there the other night,' he added in truthful afterthought. 'But that was just for fun, Mr Holmes. He doesn't - we don't make a habit of it. Just the once, with Guy, for fun. Truly.' He stared at Holmes with large, startled eyes.

'*You* do not make a habit of it I'm sure, Mr Fareham. But can you answer for your friend?'

'I can answer for his character, sir,' said Max firmly. Holmes shook his head sadly. Such loyalty to such an object!

'You have of course known him well, Mr Fareham. But I must ask you to examine your *recent* dealings with him. I believe you will find that there's been a change. I myself have encountered him at his work, and I fear that his purposes are indeed open to question.'

'But not *blackmail*, Mr Holmes!' cried Max. His eyes had filled with tears. He could not believe it. Mr Holmes spoke so gravely, and, it seemed, with such sympathy for himself. For a moment he was rocked with the ghastly impression that the world as he knew it was collapsing around him.

'I'm sorry Mr Fareham,' Mr Holmes was saying; 'There can be very little doubt.'

'But Guy would never! He just wouldn't! There

must be some appalling mistake!'

Holmes rose from his seat. He took a turn about the room. He was disturbed by the young man's distress, uncomfortably moved by the appeal of his golden, tear-filled eyes. He was also driven, reluctantly but inexorably, to consider the possibility that he might be mistaken.

He paused by the basket chair and looked down at the dark, bowed head. He laid a hand gently on the hunched shoulder. Max looked up in wonder.

'If that is the case, Mr Fareham,' said Holmes slowly, 'then rest assured that my continued investigation will reveal it to be such. Please be assured that I always check every fact. But tell your friend that he must make an honest and full confession if he wishes to save himself from the worst of accusations.'

There was a long, thoughtful silence. After a while Max rose, holding his hat and looking dazed. He faced Mr Holmes and nodded.

'Yes. Yes, I will tell him. Thank you, sir. Thank you.'

Holmes patted him on the arm. Max swayed slightly.

'Good day to you then, Mr Fareham.'

'Good day, Mr Holmes.'

Max walked mechanically to the door, pausing to look back with amazed and troubled eyes. Holmes inclined his head with a slightly puzzled smile.

Max found his way out onto the street, feeling the pressure of that hand on his shoulder, the pat on his arm. He turned his face homewards; a face wild and white with shock, and with the conflict and agitation of his heart.

Guy waited anxiously by the window. He strained to see down the street. There was no sign of Max. No sign. It seemed hours since he'd left. He wandered to the middle of the room and stood there, at a loss. He'd knocked back three brandies since Dr Watson left, and still the shock was coursing through his veins. He'd had no idea it was all so serious! Oh, he'd do anything to retrieve that time and live it over again so he could rise triumphant above temptation! Or better still, if he could just have the conversation with his mother again, and confess. It could have been a beautiful scene: him kneeling at her feet, golden and penitent, begging for forgiveness ... actually, he might still have to do just that.. Perhaps he should practise, to be sure of striking the right note. He knelt down upon the carpet and clasped his hands in supplication, but the absence of a floor-length mirror in which to appreciate the tableau rendered the exercise somewhat redundant.

He rose with a sigh, and began to pace to and fro. Oh, well – at least he had the money. Dear, good, kindly Doctor Watson! He was beginning to feel a little less anxious, a little more cheerful. The brandy was doing its work at last. He sauntered round the room, congratulating himself yet again on its unique aesthetic presentation.

Suddenly he stopped in his tracks and clapped a hand to his forehead. What a prize fool he was! He'd always had the wherewithal to raise the money, right here in this room! That little ivory box on the mantelpiece, for instance, could well be worth a hundred alone. And that vase, perched high on display - what had the man called it? Ning, Ming? Anyway as Max had pointed out, it was probably a priceless antique! He reached up on tiptoe and took it down to examine. He flicked it with his finger, and was pleased by its clear chime. He peeped inside.

How strange! There was a small packet of papers - thin, crackly papers of the sort he'd seen architects use when drawing up plans - tucked deep inside. He fished them out gingerly, extracted them from their wrapping, and spread them out upon the table: two large sheets, covered in diagrams and mathematical formulae. What a strange thing! Perhaps *they* were worth something. This could be some ancient Chinese manuscript ... but no, there was a faded red stamp in the corner that appeared to say *WAR OFFICE*. How odd! Perhaps some old buffer who'd owned the vase before him had tossed them in absent-mindedly one day at the War Office, or stashed them out of sight when a red-faced General marched in and surprised him. He must have completely forgotten where he'd put them! Guy laughed aloud. He turned the papers over, and soon became absorbed in calculating the value of his various *objets d'art*.

Max found him deeply preoccupied, biting the end of his pencil whilst scrutinising a page of scribbled calculations.

'Good news, Maxy!' he shouted, looking up. 'I'm in the clear. If I sell all the stuff listed here, with the money I got out of Dr Watson it should cover everything! I can get back the diamonds and pay off all the rest into the bargain! What a fool I was not to think of it before!'

Max laid his hat upon the table and sat down, scrutinising his friend's face gravely.

'What money from Dr Watson?'

'Oh, I forgot. I had the most stupendous brainwave after you'd gone. I summoned the dear Doctor to me, and touched him for a hundred. Superb, eh? And of course it left the coast clear for you.'

'What?' Max frowned. 'Why on earth would Dr Watson give you money?'

Guy could not resist. 'Oh, you know. He just couldn't say no to me, Maxy. I whistled, and he coughed up. Easy.'

Max's eyes widened. 'You mean he gave you all that money just because you made eyes at him?'

'Well, no, not quite. I suppose I did pile on the pressure, in a way. I was very good, though. I surpassed myself. What's up, Maxy?'

Max's face was wooden with shock. Guy forged ahead regardless.

'Anyway, how was Mr Holmes? You know, I've been so busy being sensible and domestic that I'd almost forgotten - what did he say?'

'He said,' said Max slowly, 'That you're going to have to make a full confession if you're to wriggle clear.'

'Wriggle clear?' repeated Guy delightedly, 'Did he really use that expression?'

Max clicked his tongue. 'No, of course not. I can't remember what expression he used. But he was very severe, Guy; very, very severe.'

'I thought you looked a bit done in. Was he dreadfully harsh? I can imagine him being quite hard and cruel, you know, in the right circumstances. *Was* he hard and cruel?'

'No. He wasn't. He was very understanding, considering. But he was - well, severe. He said he abhors crimes like yours.'

'What? That's a bit strong, isn't it? Dr Watson was much nicer. Though he did say - oh God, yes, he *was* quite severe too. Why is everyone being so hard on me, Maxy? Is it because true Beauty is a challenge to the narrow-minded?'

'How can you prattle on?' cried Max angrily. He was gripped by a listless depression - a reaction to his frayed and shredded nerves - and the interview with Holmes had seared into his brain and was playing and replaying there in mortifying detail.

'Look Guy, we must talk seriously,' he said firmly. 'Mr Holmes said that this business is really bad, and that someone else is implicated, and might go to prison, or worse. I've been thinking about it all the way home. Do you think your poor mother could be charged with fraud, or gross misconduct or something?'

Guy looked horrified. 'What? Why would Mother be charged with - oh, you mean the diamond swap!

How does he know about that? Oh, he must think the entire family is degenerate!'

'He didn't say *who*, he just said that you'd caused immense suffering and that someone else stood in danger of a prison sentence. Or Worse. You don't think Sir Edward would - you know, divorce her, do you? Wouldn't that be awful?' He bit his lip. 'And Guy, there's something else. I must say it, because it's absolutely poisonous, and I can't bear to keep it to myself. He said you'd committed blackmail!'

To his surprise, Guy blushed deeply.

'Guy! You haven't - oh, God, what have you done?'

'Oh Maxy!' wailed his friend, 'How on earth did he find out? I didn't think anyone would ever know!'

Max watched Guy's face in astonishment. 'What? What is it?'

'Oh. Oh!' cried Guy, 'What an awful person he must think me! It's so vile!'

'*What* is so vile? What?'

'Oh God. I suppose I must tell all, now. Oh, how I rue the day! Oh that this too, too solid flesh would -'

'Guy!!'

'Yes, yes. It was Atkinson. He threw me in the fountain. You remember. He used to hang around with that vile Manderville fellow. Anyway, I caught them both in the Dean's rooms one day when I'd gone up for a tutorial. They were cribbing the questions for the final exams. And I - well, after all those things they'd said about me, threatening to go to the Dean and have me sent down, and all that - and there they were, caught in the act, doing something ten times worse! And I just can't bear hypocrisy, you know that Maxy. So I made them let me in on it.'

Max looked appalled. 'Guy! I *thought* you'd done remarkably well, considering how little you'd studied all year. That was terribly dishonourable.'

'I know.' Guy hung his head, and sniffed penitently. 'And now Mr Holmes has found me out, and he'll expose me to every ignominy. Though he can't actually have me sent down now that I *am* down, can he?'

Max did not answer. He was lost in thought.

'Wait a moment.' He shook Guy by the shoulder. 'That can't be it. That was months ago. Mr Holmes seemed to think this was something recent, to do with your debts. What else have you done, Guy?' He tried to sound as coldly deliberate as Mr Holmes. 'Have you been going out on the streets on your own?'

Guy looked up. 'What? Well, of course I've been out on my own,' he said sharply. 'Do I need a chaperone, or something? I can't waste money on cabs every time I want to leave the house!'

'No, no. I mean where we went together, last night. Like *that* is what I mean.'

Guy sniffed, and looked blank. 'Well, no. Does Mr Holmes think I should?'

Max sighed heavily. 'Don't be an idiot. Do you promise me solemnly that you have *never* been on the streets and actually - you know. And that you haven't ever blackmailed anyone in that way.'

Guy's mouth fell open in astonishment; then he

pulled himself together, and tried to look dignified. 'I *think* I can just about make out what you're implying, Max, and I can assure you I've never done anything of the sort! What do you take me for?'

He paused, and seemed suddenly struck by something. 'Do you know, Dr Watson said something about going on the streets, and I couldn't make head nor tail of it. So *he* thinks - and *you* think, and Mr Holmes thinks - oh no, it's too awful!' His face crumpled again, and he buried it in his hands. 'Oh, I'm ruined for life!'

'No of course you're not, if you haven't *done* it. It can't be as serious as Mr Holmes thinks it is.' Max's voice was puzzled.

'But then,' said Guy in a small voice, 'I didn't think I could be hanged for borrowing Mother's jewels, either.'

'What?'

'That's what Dr Watson said!' He sniffed loudly.

'Oh Lord,' said Max. He sat mute for some minutes, the silence punctuated by the occasional violent sniff from Guy.

'Now, look here,' he said finally, 'There's obviously been some dreadful mistake. I'm certain you can't possibly be hanged for pawning your mother's jewellery. And I'm pretty sure *she* couldn't go to prison for playing about with her own property.'

Guy looked at Max with hope shining through his tears. Max tried desperately to think, toying with the paper on which Guy had done his messy sums.

'Let's try and work this out. There's got to be

another factor somewhere. Here, pass me that pencil and we'll write it all down. What's all this?' He had turned the paper over, and was looking at the abstruse calculations and intricate diagrams that covered the other side.

'Don't know,' said Guy huffily.

'Well, where did you get it?'

'It was stuffed in that vase - that Chinese thing up there. I fished it out. It must've been in there for donkey's years.'

'Don't be silly, Guy - the dealer would have noticed. Besides' - he tapped the corner - 'it's dated here: *March 1890*. That's less than six months ago.'

'Ah, well. It still somehow got hidden in my vase.'

Max scrutinised the plans. 'It says *WAR OFFICE* in this corner!'

'Mmm. Yes. I saw that.'

Max looked at Guy for a long moment; he opened his mouth to speak, and then shut it again.

Guy giggled. 'You look like a fish!'

'I think,' said Max very slowly, 'that we might have something really important here. I think we should put it somewhere safe for a bit.'

'Oh but Max, it's got all my calculations on the back of it! Anyway, if it were all *that* important the Government would be after it by now, wouldn't they? We'd have Scotland Yard on our doorstep.'

Max's face flushed suddenly, then went very white. His eyes were enormous.

'Guy,' he whispered, 'Oh God, Guy, I think we may just have found the missing factor.'

He looked at the plans for a long time, then laid them down reverently.

'Oh, good heavens,' he murmured, clutching the edge of the table.

'But I tell you, Holmes, nothing could have been more pathetic than the sight of that young man when I pointed out the seriousness of his situation as you'd outlined it to me!' Dr Watson spoke with emphasis, gesturing with his cigarette.

'Yes, yes,' murmured his companion. The room was filled with smoke. Holmes had obviously been thinking over his cases since Max Fareham's departure, and the atmosphere bore witness to his preference for strong black shag; Watson had added the lighter smoke of a cigarette to the mix.

Holmes said no more, and seeing this Watson tried to press his advantage.

'He was shocked like one who has no inkling of what he has done. Holmes, I don't believe he actually has anything to do with the blackmail case. He thought I was talking about the diamonds the whole time. I must have your permission to explain things to him! I feel personally responsible. I should have been more discreet I know, but he insisted on making this rather vague confession to me, and I assumed -'

'Yes, yes my dear Watson, I grieve both for your indiscretion and for your wounded conscience, but please, spare me.' Holmes spoke sharply, then stopped abruptly.

'I'm sorry, my dear fellow.' He laid down his pipe and put a listless hand to his head. 'I have not fared much better with young Mr Fareham than you did with Clements, so set your conscience at ease. I have been on the wrong track, just as you say. There's been a singular series of coincidences at work here - just do me the favour of sitting quietly while I try to assess the facts.'

Watson, ever willing to make allowances for his friend, sat back to listen.

'On the one hand,' said Holmes tapping the arm of his chair with a long index finger, 'We have the positive identification by the blackmail victim. He was adamant that my detailed description of Guy Clements matched that of his blackmailer. What can we weigh against that? That the man is in a sorry state of anxiety and eager to find and punish his persecutor. Any similarity in colouring and feature would be enough to suggest a complete likeness to the mind of such an individual. Now, what have I learned from my investigations on the streets where the blackmailer operates? Yes, there is a young man of that description at work. Yes, he is on the streets several nights a week.' Holmes frowned, leaning forward to rest his elbows on his knees with fingers steepled at his forehead. 'The only young man I find answering that description is - Guy Clements. Why should he be there? Just for fun, as his friend insists? Is not that an extraordinary co-incidence?'

Watson sighed. 'It is indeed. But stranger things have happened, Holmes.'

'True, my dear fellow. The world is full of odd chances, and the most commonplace events are the products of infinitesimal probabilities, as I have often remarked.'

He fell silent for a moment. 'Go on, Holmes,' prompted Watson gently.

'Ah yes. My attempts to locate the missing set of papers have thrown up another connection.' Holmes reached for his pipe and paused to relight it. 'With the help of my Irregulars I think I can name the agent involved - Wiggins tells me that the slippery customer currently known as Louis la Rothière has been more than usually active recently. He has had recent, clandestine meetings with two or three embassy representatives. This in itself proves nothing, of course; but crucially, he also reports that a young man has visited La Rothière on several occasions. A blond young man, slightly built, and cautious. Knowing that gentleman's tastes it is unlikely that these visits are designed to combine business with pleasure.' A grimace of disgust passed across Holmes' features. 'Wiggins has attempted to trace this boy, but without success. This in itself is odd. Rarely has he failed me.

'So it looks, Watson, as though the key to the papers' whereabouts lies either with La Rothière or with this elusive unknown whose identity, if we are to discount Guy Clements, remains an enigma. A search of La Rothière's residence must come first I think. We will find further clues there.'

Holmes' keen eyes narrowed, and he drummed his fingers impatiently on the chair arm. Watson saw that he had completely forgotten his request for permission to explain their joint mistake to Guy.

'But Holmes,' he said urgently, 'I really do think we owe Clements a visit before we go anywhere else. Do you know, I believe that young man genuinely thought he was in danger of the noose when I'd finished with him! His complete ignorance of the law and exaggerated view of his own misdeed actually made it seem possible! I don't believe I can rest until we put him out of his misery in the matter.'

Holmes refocussed upon his friend with apparent difficulty.

'Yes,' he said calmly; then, 'So to be clear, Watson, you are completely convinced of his innocence?'

'I am, Holmes,' said Watson firmly. 'I do not believe Guy Clements capable of the sustained villainy you've described. And when you have met him you will, I'm sure, agree.'

'No doubt,' said Holmes drily. 'Max Fareham was most eloquent on that score. I deliberately kept the matter vague, in the hope that he would reveal knowledge one way or the other. In retrospect I can clearly see that his conversation referred only to the diamond theft; which accounts, by the way, for his talk of *fakes* and *copies* - an explanation for the reticence of Lady Esher. He appears to know nothing of the other matter.'

'Indeed, Holmes. And I believe that the same of Clements.'

Holmes nodded slowly. 'Very well then, Watson. I agree.' He rose, knocked out his pipe, and stretched.

'The diamond theft could itself be said to weigh in Clements' favour, for why should someone capable of blackmail and treachery risk his reputation on the most amateurish piece of domestic pilfering I've encountered in a long while? No Watson, our blond young man is a much more formidable customer than Guy Clements. I look forward to meeting him. But first, as you suggest, we'll tidy up the matter of the diamonds with a visit to your young friend's house.'

Watson's expressions of relief and approval were drowned out by a sudden fit of coughing as Holmes struggled to open a window.

'Good heavens, Watson,' he said when he could speak. 'Your filthy habits have made this chamber unfit for habitation! Pray ring for our boots, and let's get out into the fresh air.'

'Where shall I put them, Maxy?' Guy was holding a necklace up to the light, watching the facets sparkle. 'Pretty, aren't they? They're terribly good copies, you know. *I* certainly couldn't tell them apart.'

'I don't see why you should expect to,' said Max languidly from the couch, putting aside the newspaper he had been reading. 'I never heard that you were an expert in precious stones.'

'Do they suit me?' Guy was holding the jewels at his collar.

'They go splendidly with the silk cravat, Guy, but not with the green carnation.'

Guy crowed with delight. 'So you *have* noticed! I collected it from the florist on the way back. I thought you'd be as blind as a bat, and I'd have to point it out to you. And guess what, I've got one for you too!'

'Wait, wait, wait!' laughed Max; 'Just put those jewels away first!'

Guy threw the necklace at his friend, who caught it awkwardly, and rushed out of the room. It was a beautiful thing, thought Max, lying back on the couch to examine the fake diamonds at leisure.

Suddenly there was a ring at the door; he sat up hurriedly and looked round for a hiding place. Guy's Ming vase again! What better place, while awkward guests were entertained? Max crossed to the mantelpiece, reached up, and dropped the necklace in; the vase rang gently as the stones struck the side.

He turned quickly to the mirror to smooth his hair and compose himself. A worried frown was on his face; it was nearly half past six, and his plans for sobering Guy down and taking him, the War Office documents and the necklace round to Baker Street to get everything sorted out as quickly as possible would have to be put on hold if the call proved to be an extended one. He hoped it would not be Lady Esher again; he did not think he could bear another fraught interview, especially if Guy took his time about owning up...

The door opened, and Guy entered. In one hand he clutched a small box containing a carnation tinted absinthe green; with the other, he ushered their visitors into the room.

Max's heart jumped violently, and he felt the blood surge to his face. First came Dr Watson, looking as kindly as ever, and then, just behind him, came Mr Holmes. The memory of their earlier meeting was too fresh for him to be able to greet that austere figure with equanimity. He felt his blush deepen as he met Holmes' grey gaze; he hoped he saw the hint of a smile there.

'... so delighted to see you both!' Guy was saying, standing relaxed and graceful in the middle of the room as though oblivious to the fact that one of his guests suspected him of blackmail and treachery while he owed the other a hundred pounds. Max bit his lip in embarrassment.

'Such a lot has happened since I saw you, Dr Watson, and I really think I can explain everything. I feel so much better now.'

He rang the bell for the maid. 'Please do sit down, both of you. Oh Mr Holmes, it's utterly thrilling to meet you at last! I've heard so much about you from Max ...'

Max thought he detected a wheedling, nervous tone to his friend's voice; he did have some shame, then. He would have snorted derisively had he not wished to appear as dignified and adult as possible.

'The pleasure is mutual Mr Clements,' said Holmes, seating himself gracefully in the dragon-legged chair. He looked watchful, as though expecting some particular reaction on Guy's part.

Max could have told him that Guy delighted in flouting the rules of expected behaviour on every possible occasion; and this, it appeared was to be just such an occasion.

'You must excuse me for a moment,' he said gaily, 'I have something here for Max that just won't wait!'

He turned to Max and presented the poisonous-looking green flower with a flourish. Max regarded it with dread.

'Put it on, Maxy! Oh here, let me.' He fastened the decoration deftly onto Max's lapel. 'There. Now you look quite the thing. Doesn't he, Dr Watson?'

Guy turned to Watson with a charming smile, and the Doctor looked vaguely alarmed.

'A most interesting buttonhole, Mr Clements,' he said gruffly. Mr Holmes, Max noticed, was resting his chin on his hand so that his mouth was hidden.

'Thank you, Guy,' he said in warning tones, escaping to the sofa and hoping the theatricals were now exhausted; but to his horror Guy came to sit beside him, and actually ruffled his hair. His friend was obviously jealous, and determined to embarrass him.

'Max is so sweet!' laughed Guy; 'You'd never guess what his shyness conceals, would you Mr Holmes?'

'I have often found the most surprising traits concealed behind the face presented to the world, Mr Clements,' said Holmes calmly, looking at him very directly.

Mary the housemaid appeared at the door. 'Yes, sir?' she said.

'Tea, please,' said Guy, 'Or would you prefer something stronger, gentlemen? Of course you would! Cancel the tea, er, Mary.'

She curtsied, and was about to leave when her eye fell upon Mr Holmes. She glared at him, and went very white; Max noticed that Holmes regarded her with equal concentration as she turned on her heel and left the room. Guy had noticed it too.

'Extraordinary things, servants,' he said, going over to the sideboard and assembling four tumblers. 'That girl is particularly insolent. I shall get rid of her.'

He poured generous measures of brandy and handed them to his guests with a winning smile.

Dr Watson and Max drank gratefully; Holmes put his glass down on the occasional table, and fixed his eyes once more upon Guy. Guy met the detective's cool gaze happily; then suddenly his expression changed, betraying puzzlement and a hint of alarm.

'Er - have we met before, Mr Holmes?' he asked cautiously; 'Apart from on your doorstep, I mean. I'm sure we - I mean, I'm sure I - your face looks very familiar...'

Holmes' smile betrayed a hint of wryness. 'Why yes, Mr Clements,' said courteously. 'We have, as you say, met before, and very recently. Last night, in fact. At about two o'clock in the morning.'

Max suppressed a yelp of astonishment, and Guy jumped visibly.

'Oh!' he said; then added in a small, placatory voice, 'Your Italian is very good sir, if I may say so.'

'Thank you, Mr Clements. And I in turn congratulate you on your original rendition of Gluck's masterpiece.'

Dr Watson raised a puzzled eyebrow; Guy gave a pale imitation of his usual winning smile.

'Thank you sir,' he said, in subdued tones.

'And now,' said Holmes, sitting back in his chair, 'I think we are in a position to get down to business.'

Max licked his lips. 'Mr Holmes, before you go on, I think there's been the most awful misunderstanding.'

'Indeed,' said Holmes pleasantly. 'That is why we have come.'

'Oh,' said Max. He'd been preparing himself to engage in a painful battle on behalf of the one he loved with the one he most admired. Now the wind had been taken from his sails, and he shut his mouth feeling rather foolish.

Holmes looked kindly upon him. 'Your visit to me this afternoon, Mr Fareham, and my friend Watson's visit to you, Mr Clements, have indeed thrown certain aspects of this situation into strange relief. But before I proceed, I must have an assurance from both of you that you will answer my questions with complete frankness. Will you do that?'

Max and Guy nodded in unison. Watson had to suppress a smile. They looked so young, and so anxious to please: the one perched on the edge of the sofa, his hair golden in the sunlight, a faint blush upon his smooth cheek; the other sitting forward, attentive and graceful, his brown eyes serious as he clasped his knees with dark, slender hands. On the lapels of their jackets glowed their foolish green flowers.

Holmes sighed, and paused for a moment. He appeared to collect his thoughts. Than he fixed his eyes on the mantelpiece, and his austere white face assumed its far-away look as he began to speak.

Madeleine was as near to panicking as she had ever come. It was him - no doubt whatsoever. She knew him by description, knew him minutely. She'd made it her business to know him. What was he doing here?

She rubbed at the silver knife she was cleaning, noting a tiny dint in the handle. The kitchen was empty but the atmosphere was close. Cook was gossiping with someone at the tradesman's door, brushing tiny black flies from her hot face, not hurrying to prepare a dinner tonight - Mr Clements and Mr Fareham were going out, and the household would eat when they'd left.

She looked at the kitchen clock; it was nearly seven. Another hour, and she could leave. Could she risk going up to the drawing room, as she'd planned? Would the papers still be there? Would *he* still be there? How much did he know? And *why was he here?*

Madeleine moaned under her breath and unconsciously pressed her forehead, leaving traces of cleaning paste to dry there, china white. Her fingers were covered with it. It cracked around the joints, snaked into minute polygons near her thumbs. She wanted to wash it off, wash everything off ... she had to get away. With a muffled chime, she threw the knife down onto the thick linen cloth.

She moved towards the door. Perhaps she could

say she was ill? She actually felt ill ... Go home early, just this once, Mrs Preston?

The air was heavy with foreboding. There was a storm coming.

Yes. Her instincts propelled her like pistons. Forget about the drawing room; get out of the house. Go now, while you still can.

'So it's agreed, then,' said Holmes leaning back in his chair. 'You yourself will return the diamonds, Mr Clements.'

Guy nodded quickly.

'Good. I think in any case that this is a family affair in which my further interference would be unwelcome - especially since you say the gems are copies. It will be for you to decide whether to broach that line of conversation with your mother.' He smiled. 'Personally, I'd advise letting the matter lie.'

'Yes sir,' said Guy. 'I think I will. Everyone's entitled to a skeleton or two, and Mother's must be so ancient by now. It's not worth picking over old bones, is it?' He sat back against Max's shoulder and pulled out his cigarette case. His hands were trembling; Mr Holmes' questions had been both astute and direct.

'Good,' said Holmes again. 'Then it only remains for me to apologise for suspecting you in certain other matters. As it is, Mr Clements, I hope you will have learned something from your troubles.'

They fell silent for a moment, and Holmes now sipped at the brandy which had lain untasted on the table while he posed his questions. Guy rose hastily, and offered him a cigarette.

'Thank you,' he said, accepting. 'Alexandrian, I see; a distinctive make. Be careful where you drop your ash, Mr Clements, should you plan any more risque activities; I will have no trouble in tracing its source.'

Guy laughed nervously.

'Well,' said Holmes after another short silence, 'Thank you for your hospitality under rather stressful circumstances.' He finished his drink and looked at Watson, preparing to leave.

Max pulled himself together quickly. He put down his glass and reached inside his jacket for his pocket book. 'There is something else, Mr Holmes,' he said urgently.

Holmes looked at him, and raised an eyebrow.

'Yes, sir.' Max nodded emphatically. 'It's to do with your other investigation. At least, I think it is. The missing papers.'

'Missing papers, Mr Fareham?' Holmes' voice was non committal, and Max realised that he'd made a blunder.

'I - well, Dr Watson -' he continued in some confusion, for he could not retract what he had said and besides, it was important. '- er, he mentioned you were investigating some missing Government papers, and I assume that this is what you suspected Guy of exhorting through blackmail.'

Guy sniffed loudly, and looked from Max to Holmes with a mixture of aggrieved innocence and avid curiosity. Max avoided his gaze. He noted that Dr Watson was examining his shoes with sudden interest, but he was determined to gain at least a glimmer of respect from Mr Holmes' cold grey eyes.

'Well, I think I may have them here,' he said,

fumbling with his pocket book and extracting the papers which were neatly folded inside. He rose, and handed them to Holmes.

Holmes took them, but did not look at them. He looked instead at Max.

'Pray continue, Mr Fareham,' he said very softly.

'Guy found them,' began Max. 'They were -'

'Oh, *those!* Oh, you must let me have them back for a moment, Mr Holmes. They have my financial affairs set out in alarming detail on the back. I really think I should erase them before that old buffer gets his hands on them.'

Holmes raised both eyebrows.

'I mean,' added Guy, seeing his expression, 'The old buffer in the War Office who tossed them into my expensive vase.'

Holmes sighed and rested his chin on his hand. He cast a look of appeal at Max.

'Guy means that he found the papers in that vase, sir.' Max indicated the ornament. 'And he doesn't know how they got there.'

Holmes slowly unfolded the papers and examined them. Then he looked again at Max, with keen interest. Max blushed.

'This is ... very singular,' murmured Holmes, frowning. 'Quite remarkably so, in fact.'

He turned to Guy. 'When exactly did you make this fortuitous discovery, Mr Clements?'

'Oh, just this afternoon! I was totting up the value of some of my bits and pieces, seeing as my pecuniary difficulties have led me into all sorts of scrapes -' he smiled graciously at Holmes and Dr Watson - 'and there they were.'

Holmes looked at him steadily.

'Oh but Mr Holmes, it's *true!'* cried Guy, his smile vanishing in sudden alarm. 'Really it is, and I had *no idea* there were in there! I didn't even know what they were until Max pointed it out. I thought they were Chinese, or something. Ask Max. Tell him, Maxy!'

'Really, sir,' said Max earnestly, 'That's exactly how it happened. I came back from visiting you, and found Guy doing all these calculations on the back of the plans, and he honestly had no idea what they were or where they'd come from. It was I who thought they might have some connection with - all these misunderstandings. I wondered - I thought you might already know they were hidden here, and that was why you suspected Guy.'

Holmes studied the wide eyes and eager face and was once again convinced, though his expression remained guarded.

'Well, Mr Fareham,' he said, 'I must congratulate you on your quick thinking. And you were one step ahead of me - I had no reason to believe the plans were hidden in this house. The fact that they were, however, is extremely interesting and opens up a whole new set of possibilities.'

He tapped his thin lips with his forefinger while his eyes rested on Max with - yes, there *was* a gleam of admiration there. Max glowed. He had his reward.

'And you have no idea how long these papers have

been in the vase?' Holmes turned his attention back to the plans.

'Not a clue,' shrugged Guy.

'And who, may I ask, has access to this room, apart from yourselves?'

'Oh. There's Mother, of course. Don't think it was her, though. There's my stepfather – he probably knows all those buffers at the War Office. I say, do you think it might be him?'

Guy had become quite animated. Max frowned at him. 'Servants,' he said.

Mr Holmes nodded. 'Tell me about them.'

'Can't say, really,' said Guy dismissively. 'You'd better ask John about all that sort of thing. But I shouldn't imagine any of *them* are going to have access to Government secrets.'

Holmes smiled distantly. 'Do you have any objection to my questioning your domestic staff, Mr Clements?'

'Not in the least. But I say, I've had an idea! Maxy and I were going to dine at the Cafe Royal later – why don't you and Dr Watson join us? After you've done all your questioning, of course.'

Holmes gave a wry smile. 'That is very kind of you, Mr Clements, but I'm afraid the Doctor and I have work to do. Is your man downstairs? Good. This shouldn't take too long.'

Madeleine leaned into the horse-chestnut tree, drawing comfort from its strength and stillness. It was dark now. She could allow herself to relax, just a little. She'd been standing motionless for hours, clenching and unclenching her hands and gnawing her underlip raw.

At just after seven, she'd begged leave to go. By half past eight, John *(Mr Arkwright to you, Mary)* had come out and whistled for a cab, which that bastard and his friend had driven off in. Just after nine, Mr Clements and *his* friend had emerged, all poshed up, and walked off down the street arm in arm. They'd been gone for an hour now - the bells across town had just rung ten. Every quarter had been rung, each hour uncoiling slowly to its chime.

Another hour passed, quarter by quarter. Madleine pulled her shawl closely around her; it was getting cold.

The kitchen door opened, and light flooded the area; Sarah came out to the bins, and hurried back in again. A few minutes later the lights were extinguished, and the area was a pool of darkness. Now they were all going to bed, and the gents wouldn't be back 'til the early hours. She made herself wait until another quarter had been rung.

It was now, or never. Madeleine flitted lightly across the street and noiselessly opened the area gate.

She descended the steps and approached the kitchen window. She knew the latch, its weakness; had noticed it with the unconscious alertness of a practised eye. She pushed the frame with her small hand, slipped a steel hatpin through the crack, and raised the latch deftly.

The kitchen smelled of roast chicken. Tomorrow's lunch - cold fowl, she noted automatically. It was dark, but she knew every obstacle. She took a small, sharp knife from the block as she passed.

She felt a bolt of power rush through her. The house was hers - she could take it, rip it to shreds, score the mahogany and gouge the wallpaper ... but no. Business first and foremost. Up the dim stairs - a gaslight burned in the hall, so the gents wouldn't trip over their precious drunken feet when they tottered home. She flattened herself against the wall and peeped into the drawing room.

A lamp had been left burning there also, turned down low; the air was redolent of tobacco and spirits as she entered softly and approached the mantelpiece. The heavy chair creaked as she stood upon it to reach the vase. Tip it up, and -

Hard, cold in her palm! She gasped with the shock of it, as bright stones flashed in the rays from the lamp. What the hell was going on? A joke? A trap? She clutched at the mantelpiece, and made a sweep of the room, staring into the shadowy corners. Nothing stirred.

Get out, then. Get out quick.

She slipped noiselessly down from the chair and

back into the below-stairs gloom. She slid out through the window and scuttled off into the night, the fake diamonds hidden in her bosom.

Well. This is interesting.

Louis la Rothière tapped a well-manicured finger on the silver knob of his cane. He sipped his wine and turned his attention momentarily to the rest of the company, letting his gaze make a sweep of the Domino Room. Each lion had his court, and was holding forth to his courtiers. The tall, gilded mirrors reflected the animated or languid pose, the flushed or waxen face; dark suits with flashes of colour at neck and buttonhole; a lady's hat, bright as a poppinjay, nodding in agreement at some pithy remark; waiters threading their way briskly between marble-topped tables. The voices rolled over him, vehement, bored, confidential; some melodic, some harsh, but all with something to say. The Cafe Royal was at its best tonight.

Louis lit a cigar, and leaned back to listen to the two young men he'd arranged, all unbeknownst to themselves, to meet here. A quiet word with the *maitre d'hotel* and a small bribe had easily procured him a glimpse at the bookings register ...

Their conversation was conducted for the most part in undertones, but Louis had a discerning ear. Young Mr Clements, it seemed, had been involved in some amusing escapade; his dark friend was berating him affectionately for an indiscretion. He watched them in the mirror: Clements was flushed but happy, with relief in his posture and a twinkle in his eyes; the friend had a golden tint to his skin, and a serious brown gaze. A happy couple, certainly; those with a taste for that sort of thing would find them charming. Louis merely found them interesting specimens, slightly contemptible in their foolish vanity and exhibitionism - did they not know that they and their kind were teetering on the edge of an abyss? It was only a matter of time; one more Cleveland Street, one more high profile arrest, and there'd be fire and brimstone raining down, a panic-stricken exodus with the tardy entombed in pillars of salt. Louis nonchalantly adjusted his position, turning an ear in the young men's direction.

'- but you don't think,' Clements was saying with exaggerated horror, 'that he actually suspected me *again?*'

'I don't know,' came the calmer response. 'But you must admit that from his point of view, it *would* look -' His voice was lost in hubbub from the table to their left. Louis blew smoke impatiently. 'If he *had* done, it would've taken more than just my assurances to persuade him,' he heard when the burst of laughter had subsided.

'Don't be absurd,' protested Clements. 'He thinks you're absolutely -' the voice dropped and then rose shrilly - ' he *does,* it's perfectly obvious!'

A few low remarks were exchanged, followed by a burst of laughter from both. Clements' friend looked hot but pleased, shaking his head disparagingly.

So there they are, thought Louis; relieved of some burden, obviously. And with not the least suspicion that my little Pierrot has a hidey-hole right under their noses, in the bosom of a careless, hedonistic household. He indulged in a mental sneer at the ease with which the spoilt offspring of the leisure classes could be outwitted by an urchin from the streets. His features remained as bland and inscrutable as ever.

A waiter approached and began to clear away the remains of their entrees. Another hovered, ready to serve the main course. Time, thought Louis, to be on my way.

If tonight went well, he'd have no further need of Peterkin. He'd be able to clinch a lucrative deal with his Embassy contact without recourse to a middle man, and then make himself scarce. A pleasant holiday somewhere... Paris, perhaps...

He finished his wine, rose, and left without looking back; a dapper, upright figure perfectly at ease, making his way unnoticed out of the Domino Room.

Sherlock Holmes sat hunched in the corner of a hansom, his abstracted gaze sliding over the late night crowds that thronged the streets. Dr Watson stifled a yawn, and cast a sideways glance at his companion; he could read annoyance in every line of his posture. No need to ask what was preoccupying his thoughts …

They'd spent a most unprofitable few hours, driving to Vauxhall to observe the house, conducting an exasperating interview with the girl's mother, and now coming all the way back with a brief stop off at the telegraph office and no evening meal. Mrs Peterson had been impossible to communicate with - obviously a drunkard of long standing, she was only dimly aware of events unfolding around her and reality was reprocessed to suit her fancy. At one point she'd asserted that Madeleine - for that, she insisted, was the girl's real name - would soon be leaving Clements' employ for a lucrative career on the Music Hall circuit! Her daughter could earn more as a male impersonator, she said, than she'd ever done working as a skivvy; a rather startling fantasy in Watson's view, though Holmes had appeared to note it with interest. At no point did she seem to find it remarkable that the girl was not at home.

She'd also expressed surprise that they should be so persistent in their enquiries after her *daughter* when her *son,* Michael, was "such an 'andsome, obligin' young man." Holmes, visibly taken aback by the insinuation, had tried to probe her on the subject without success; all they could glean was that the son was also absent from home. They'd come away depressed by the sordidness of the house, and the life stagnating there amidst the gin bottles.

Watson yawned again. 'Holmes,' he said, unable to prevent a peevish note form creeping into his voice, 'Where are we going *now*?'

Holmes pulled his brooding gaze from the street.

'Where do *you* think we should go, Watson?' he asked mildly. 'And if you cannot supply a reasoned suggestion, then I despair of you utterly.'

'Well, let's see,' said the Doctor, pulling himself together and putting all thoughts of food and home firmly to the back of his mind; 'You've failed to find the girl whom you suspect of secreting the papers at Clements' house. She is presumably in the pay of Louis la Rothière. He will either be expecting her to bring them to him or, if she's already told him of our visit, planning to retrieve them himself.'

'Excellent so far, Watson. But why then did we go to Vauxhall? Why not straight to La Rothière's?'

'Because the girl is the weak link in the chain,' answered Watson promptly. 'Easily intimidated, or possibly seduced by La Rothière, ignorant of his profession and in all probability confused by his demands, she would have been an easier nut to crack. Am I right?'

'Not really, my dear fellow,' replied Holmes pleasantly. 'I suspect that you underestimate Miss

Madeleine Peterson quite considerably, given what her mother has let slip. But you have not yet answered my question: where should we go next?'

'Well,' said Watson, suddenly animated as his line of reasoning raced to its conclusion, 'I think we should probably go back to Clements' house and keep a watch on the place!'

Holmes chuckled, and suddenly tapped the roof of the cab. 'Stop, cabby!' he ordered; they got out, and Holmes paid the fare. He took his friend's arm and steered him away from the main road and into a quiet side street.

'Now my dear fellow, I shall sketch in a few details for you as we walk. You will observe that we are *not* going back to Clements' house. We are paying a visit to our French friend's abode. He's no more French than you are, by the way; I've more Gallic blood in my veins that he has. Anyway as you deduced, he should currently be attempting to retrieve the papers, which thanks to the clever Mr Fareham are safe in my pocketbook. He'll find a welcome waiting for him at Melville Square, however – the wire I despatched from Vauxhall was to Inspector Lestrade.'

Holmes paused to light a cigarette, shielding the flame against the warm night breeze. It lit his face starkly for an instant, and the street lamp illuminated the puff of rising smoke as it dispersed.

'Now, there is an interesting point which has obviously failed to strike you. Why would La Rothière give such a valuable set of papers to a servant girl to hide? Why would he let them out of his possession? I think we must assume that he has not yet seen or laid hands on these particular ones, but has received others – to wit, the original missing documents - and was in the process of negotiating a price with Miss Peterson. It's a long shot, but I believe the first set of papers may still be in his rooms.'

'I see,' said Watson. 'And assuming La Rothière to be from home, you are planning to make yet another unofficial entrance into a suspect's house. You're beginning to make a habit of this, Holmes; you'll be caught red-handed one of these days.'

'Well, they refuse to invite me inside in the normal way - what is the struggling investigator to do?'

Watson chuckled, then frowned as a sudden thought struck him. 'But Holmes,' he said, 'If La Rothière did not give the girl the papers, who on earth did?'

'Ah. There, Watson, you have struck upon the most interesting feature of the case. I do not believe Miss Madeleine Peterson to be the harmless dupe you have described. I think that between this young lady and her enterprising brother we have found the criminal mastermind we've been seeking. You surely noticed that although their lodgings were squalid in the extreme, the mother was attired in an expensive shawl and cap? There has been money there, Watson; possibly the children bought these presents as a sop to their consciences.'

'I don't follow, Holmes.'

Holmes clicked his tongue. 'Is it not transparent?

The boy lives off the streets, and passes his earnings and whatever else he may pick up to his sister. You saw the way she looked at me, did you not? She knew me, knew who I was and what I had come for. And if her brother resembles her, he'd fit well enough with the blackmail victim's 'fair young man'. Moreover, I think it may not be he, but girl herself who visits La Rothière incognito. Did you note how the mother accommodated the blurred awareness of having seen her daughter dressed in male attire by the drunken ingenuity of the Music Hall explanation?

'Well, if *that's* your theory,' exclaimed Watson, stopping in his tracks and pulling Holmes round to face him, 'The girl and her brother could be one and the same! This so-called 'fair young man' may not even exist!'

Holmes shook his head in exasperation. 'Really, Doctor, for a medical man ... male impersonation can only go so far, Watson. Convincing as Miss Madeleine may be, I doubt she'd pass muster working the streets. I think we must assume that the brother exists. However, it is the sister we're concerned with this evening. She'll be taken if she returns to Vauxhall, for the house is now watched; the police should also be observing Clements' house by now, and we ourselves are just yards from La Rothière's. Miss Madeleine may yet have an opportunity to prove her ingenuity.'

Louis la Rothière observed the massive and sombre form stationed beneath the horse chestnut tree; the broad glimmer of the constable's face hung in the shadows. He speculated calmly on the reason for his presence; he could, after all, be watching any one of the houses. Every few minutes he took a turn up and down to relieve his boredom. His attention wandered frequently. He probably had no knowledge of the reasoning behind his orders, and little idea of what he was guarding, or why. His burly presence was an obstacle, however, and as immoveable as an iron bar. If he *were* guarding Clements' house, it was possible that the plans had already been discovered. Louis suppressed a desire to grind his teeth as the bells across town rung yet another quarter.

He was at a loss to deduce how the police could have traced the documents to this house. Was it possible that their interest stemmed only from the minor scandal that Clements and his friend had found so amusing? Louis was not optimistic, but nor was he willing to leave the house untried. It would be good to steal a march on that arrogant guttersnipe Peterkin. He had paid well for those first papers; he suspected he had overpaid. Funds were not so copious, and he could not afford to waste money buying something that he could, with a little effort, obtain for free.

He froze into the shadows. The constable was moving off, treading heavily away down the street.

Perhaps he had several surveillance duties? But no - there was the figure of another policeman, and they had stopped to talk. The charming confidences of two men of the law; Louis thought briefly and with distaste of their undoubted banality.

This was his moment, and he took it. He moved quietly and quickly along the street by the wall, noiselessly opened the area gate and swiftly descended the steps. And yes, here was the usual ridiculous window catch; he could tell at a glance its tensile strength, its structure. He gently tested the frame and the sash shot upwards, nearly causing him to lose his balance. What incredible luck! The window had been left unfastened! A careless servant, no doubt ... Handel's *Hallelujah Chorus* played loudly in Louis' head as he stepped quietly into the kitchen.

'Look, if you're just going to go on and on at me, we might as well go home.'

'Guy. I am not going *on* at you,' said Max with threadbare patience. 'I just want you to -'

'There you go again!' expostulated Guy. He gulped at his wine. 'You're becoming awfully tedious, Max. Always wanting me to do something for the good of my soul. It's so rustic.'

'And you're getting drunk again.' Max regarded his friend with growing annoyance. Why was he being so unreasonable?

'Why are you being so unreasonable, Max?' demanded Guy, his underlip thrust forward. 'All I want is a tiny *soupcon* of fun before I grow old and grey and boring, and you jump on me like a man-eating spider.'

'There's no such thing,' said Max wearily.

'Oh, tiger then, have it your own way. You really do have a tedious and finicky regard for fact. Did you know that? You emphasise accuracy to the exclusion of all else. You have no regard for the poetic license that is the prerogative of Beauty.'

'Oh; God.' Max rolled his eyes. 'Please Guy, *please* let us not discuss aesthetics.'

'And why not, may I ask?'

'Because in the first place it's avoiding the issue, and in the second, I don't believe you actually have the first idea what you're talking about.'

Max was beginning to lose his temper. Guy had begun the evening in a boisterous frame of mind which nevertheless had been tempered by a healthy contrition. After three courses and two bottles of Chateau Lafite, the contrition had vanished and Guy's usual egotism had taken its place, vastly inflated by the sense of having been a naughty boy and got away with it. He clearly imagined himself to be a dangerous and successful criminal, with the advantage of style and looks. He'd been laying the foundations of a preposterous scheme for replacing his mother's diamonds without saying a word, and enjoying the consequent mystification.

'Please *listen* to me, Guy,' Max continued, enunciating carefully. 'You're trying to act the giddy goat again. Can't you see that it's best all round if you just take the wretched things back to your mother, apologise, and leave it at that?'

'But it's *boring,* Max. It's boring. 'You,' said Guy with lofty condescension, 'do not appreciate the effects of *ennui* upon the artistic soul. I crave excitement. I crave - the abstruse cryptogram, the -'

Max laughed rudely. Guy closed his eyes slowly and continued with renewed emphasis, '- the bizarre, the *recherche*. My life is an art form.'

'Your life,' said Max loudly, 'Is a mess. The kind of mess that only a spoiled brat can make.'

'Well!' Guy's voice was shrill and angry. Heads turned, and the conversation at the neighbouring table, which had been faltering as their argument gathered momentum, failed altogether.

'I am not staying here to be insulted!' Guy rose in a lordly manner, head high and cheeks flushed. Max caught at his hand.

'Sit down, for God's sake,' he whispered savagely. 'Everyone's looking.'

Guy seated himself again, smoothing his hair ostentatiously. He'd caught a glimpse of his reflection in the tall mirror opposite, and decided that the flush on his cheeks rather suited him. He turned to Max and opened his mouth to speak. Max quickly laid a finger on his lips.

'Guy,' he said firmly, taking his hand, 'You are an absolute idiot sometimes, and you make me ill with worry, but I love you. And I want you to do one thing for me.'

Guy regarded him with haughty suspicion.

'I want you,' continued Max, 'to simply to give back the diamonds. *Please.* Let me finish. Just give them back, and then I promise we'll do something new and exciting together.'

Guy's red lips curved into a smile. 'Oh, Maxy!' he said coyly.

'Stop it. I mean we'll go away together somewhere, just the two of us. How about that?'

Guy's face became stony. 'I am *not* going to be lured into the countryside to vegetate in some decrepit old farmhouse surrounded by yokels and sheep. Not even for you, Maxy.'

'No, no. We'll go abroad somewhere. Monte Carlo - how about it?'

'*Money* is how about it, Max,' said Guy with heavy

condescension.

'Paris, then. I'll touch my old man for a bit, and you can do a few more calculations and whistle up something I'm sure ... Please, Guy. Paris. If you'll just give back the diamonds.'

Guy's lips curved upwards once more, and he inclined his head graciously.

'Paris will do nicely,' he said; then bounced up from his seat, flung his arms around Max's neck and kissed him resoundingly on the lips. 'Maxy, you're a perfect angel!' he cried.

The conversation at the next table, which had just been recovering from Guy's shriek, was now struck dumb as if by a bolt from Jehovah. The Domino Room was not, however, entirely unused to such scenes, and the majority of the regulars hardly raised an eyebrow.

'Champagne!' cried Guy, and raised his arm to summon a waiter; but Max gripped him firmly by the wrist.

'*Dearest* Guy,' he said diplomatically, 'You know that I have not got the artistic temperament, *in excelsis et profundis* and so on, and consequently, being an ordinary mortal, I do get tired at the end of an evening.'

'I'm sorry to hear that,' said Guy kindly.

'Yes. And over the course of the last twenty-four hours I've been out on the streets 'til three in the morning, had an excruciating interview with the most brilliant mind in London, discovered some stolen Government papers, seen my best friend accused of blackmail and treachery, had a lot of explaining to do at yet another excruciating interview ...'

'Yes. I see,' said Guy again, and he smiled.

'So if it wouldn't be too utterly tedious for you, do you think we could dispense with the champagne, and with the coffee and liqueurs, and just go home to bed?'

'Go home and go to bed?' Guy looked suddenly delighted at the suggestion.

'Yes. Well - yes.'

'Do you know Maxy, you're full of wonderful ideas this evening!' declared Guy, summoning the waiter for the bill.

Dr Watson was standing quietly by the door. He was alert but relaxed as he watched his friend methodically search through the contents of bureaux, draws and boxes. Monsieur la Rothière's rooms were chaste and anonymous, he noted; they were clean, neat and impersonal. There was not one sentimental ornament upon the mantelpiece, not one interesting book upon the shelves. These were the chambers of a passionless man. He wondered with amusement how a burglar would cope with Holmes' rooms at Baker Street. He'd retire hastily, he imagined, bewildered by all the mess. Come to think of it, a good turn over would probably improve the look of the place ...

'Watson.'

'Yes Holmes?' he responded with a start.

'I think we may have something.' His companion spoke in a soft, precise voice. 'If I'm not very much mistaken, this brick in the hearth has lately been disturbed. Let's see what – ah, yes, here it comes. And behold -' he gave a low chuckle - 'or *voila,* as Monsieur Louis would say...' He held up a small packet.

'Is it?'

'It most certainly is, my dear fellow.' Holmes rose and dusted the knees of his trousers. He spread out the papers on the table, turning the reading lamp upon them.

'Excellent. These are undoubtedly the first set of

missing papers; though I cannot see that they have any connection with those placed so thoughtfully in Guy Clements' vase...' He stooped over them, a slender finger following the lines of formulae and calculations. 'Neither can I see that they are of any particular importance as they stand. La Rothière obviously has no detailed knowledge of chemistry, whatever his other talents. Rather an inefficient little spy, when all is said and done.' He chuckled.

'Let us make good our exit, Watson. It's been amusing for me, but tedious for you, standing guard; though you've carried out that duty with your usual efficiency.' Holmes smiled a brief, warm smile and patted his friend's shoulder. They prepared to leave.

'*Au revoir,* Monsieur La Rothière,' murmured Holmes as his keen gaze swept the room once more. It was as though it had never been disturbed. He was about to turn out the reading lamp, when there was a ring at the front door: two short rings; a pause; one long ring.

They both froze. Holmes looked at Watson for a long moment, then motioned him to stand by the door. He put a finger to his lips and moved softly out into the passageway.

The ring was repeated, in the same pattern. Holmes stood in the unlit hallway and quietly opened the front door, flattening himself in its shadow and avoiding the dim rectangle of light from the street.

'Mister Louis?' said a quiet, gruff voice.

'*Entrez,*' said Holmes.

'Mister Louis?' A slim figure stepped across the

threshold; Holmes shot out an arm and pulled the visitor in, slamming the door shut.

'*Bonsoir,*' he said; 'I'm sorry to disappoint you -' he pulled the figure round to face him - 'Miss Madeleine Peterson, is it not? Mister Louis is not at home. Perhaps you'd care to talk to me instead.'

Madeleine's small, hard left hand had not been idle; she'd shaken free the kitchen knife concealed in her sleeve, grasped it firmly and stabbed viciously at the hand that held her wrist. She felt the blade turn on bone, and jerked it free to stab again; but a strong grip numbed her fingers, and the little weapon clattered onto the tiles. Her adversary kicked it well out of reach.

The hand that gripped her right wrist was suddenly slippery, and she broke free, hitting out as hard as she could. The panic of the night surfaced in her, and she knew she would kill and kill again to get back through that door, out into the cool safe darkness. But another presence was looming behind her, and her silent, fierce struggle came to an end as strong hands grabbed and pinioned her arms.

'Bring her through, Watson,' said the first voice.

It was him. And she had struck him one. Oh good, oh glorious - she'd felt the bone turn under her knife. If only she'd gone for the face, the throat! She laughed briefly, and then fell silent. If only she'd got his throat!

Max was already yawning when they arrived home. It was still early by Guy's standards, and he'd kept up a stream of inconsequential chatter throughout the journey. They let themselves in at the front door.

'Just one snifter before bed, Maxy. For me. You know you can refuse me nothing,' said Guy gaily.

'I was going to suggest one myself, as a matter of fact. I know you've not yet taken in the requisite quantity of alcohol.'

They stumbled into the drawing room. It was pitch dark. 'Oh, John's forgotten to leave a light on. What on earth was he thinking? I shall have to speak to him about it.'

Max stood in the doorway while Guy lit a lamp; he watched the golden glow rise up to illuminate his face. Guy turned to meet his gaze, and seemed about to speak when his expression changed to one of astonishment.

'Good grief!' he exclaimed, 'I don't think we've had the pleasure - watch out, Maxy!'

Max spun to his left just in time to avoid a blow. Before the shadowy figure could recover itself, he jumped forward and grasped it by the shoulder. Guy was suddenly beside him and together, by dint of superior weight and pure luck, they bore the man to the floor, pinioned his arms and sat upon him. There was a series of muffled oaths from their victim, to which they paid no attention. Max kicked the door shut as Guy kept up a running commentary.

'What fun! It's a burglar! Not a very good one, actually. What shall we do with him, Maxy? Should we tie him up? We'll have to wake John, and summon the police. I say, you, what's your name?'

'Pray,' said the muffled voice, 'let me sit up. You are wrenching my arm.'

'Oh, I'm awfully sorry. I should have offered you a seat, perhaps, and poured you a drink. Max, can you hit him really hard and render him unconscious?'

'Wait, wait!' pleaded the prisoner, 'Truly, I am in great pain. Please, at least shift your weight a little.'

Max looked dubiously at Guy, and ran a hand inexpertly over the man's pockets within reach. He fished out a small, black revolver from one of them, and held it gingerly, a horrified expression on his face.

'You could have shot us!' he croaked, his voice unsteady; 'I think we should summon the police, Guy, *now*. This man is dangerous.'

There were more curses, and a groan as Guy adjusted his position.

'I could not have shot you, truly, Messieurs. The gun is not loaded. Look for yourselves.'

'He's right,' said Max in surprise after a cursory inspection. 'Why do you carry it, then?'

'Oh,' moaned their captive, 'For the love of God, let me sit up. I would have threatened you with it, no more.'

'What were you after, eh? Sit on him a bit harder,

Guy, while I fetch the curtain cord.'

'I *can't* sit on him any harder than I already am,' said Guy petulantly.

'Ouf! Yes, yes, my good sir, you can. You have - ow - adroitly placed your knee on my spine!'

Max was back, tying the man's hands together with an efficient knot.

'Roll him over, Guy.'

Guy did so. 'We should tie his legs too, you know,' he said.

'We haven't anything to tie them with - unless you take off your braces,' suggested Max.

'Oh, Max! Take off your own. These are my favourites.'

'My dear sirs, use *my* braces,' offered their victim helpfully, 'Or better still, do not secure me further. There really is no need.'

'*Vous êtes francais, n'est-ce pas?*' asked Max.

'*Oui, oui, je suis francais.* But I would prefer to speak to you in English, gentlemen.'

Louis had struggled to a sitting position and was looking at them appealingly; they looked back at him, flushed and tipsy. They're just drunken schoolboys, thought Louis, gathering himself for a supreme effort. He would *not* be arrested as a common burglar.

'I bet I know what you're after,' Guy was saying, 'And you can't have them, because they're not here.'

'No,' agreed Max. 'Didn't think we'd be onto you so fast, did you? Well, let me tell you, *Monsieur le cambrioleur,* that those papers are now safely in the hands of Mr Sherlock Holmes!'

Louis' heart skipped a beat. Sherlock Holmes - this was really too dreadful. But something lent his inspiration wings, and he swiftly composed his features into an expression of joyful relief.

'*Oh mon Dieu!* Thank heaven for that! And Monsieur Holmes has taken them? Ah, he is a sharp one, though he does tend to act without consulting us.'

Max looked startled. 'Us? You know him? What do you mean by *us*?'

'Well ...' Louis looked almost coy. 'I am scarcely in a position to reveal my superiors' identity, but I can assure you, gentlemen, that the best interests of the Empire are well served by - *us*.'

'Oh,' said Max. Guy looked intrigued.

'And is Mr Holmes one of them?' he inquired pleasantly.

'One of us? *Mais oui, naturellement.* We have often worked together, dear Holmes and myself. A most brilliant mind. An incomparable operative.' (Superb, Louis! Their faces were clearing of suspicion as he watched.)

'Yes,' agreed Max, 'he is. But what are you *doing* here?'

'*Ma foi, Monsieur,*' smiled their captive, 'I was merely obeying orders. We had traced the papers to this household - you are fortunate, my dear sirs, that you were not placed in danger; you have been harbouring a most desperate spy here, all unwittingly I'm sure - and I was directed to retrieve the missing plans secretly.' He looked from Max to Guy, and back again. 'Secrecy is always preferred, gentlemen.'

Max nodded in agreement. Guy's eyes were avid.

'Desperate spy?' he repeated in awed tones. 'Who? Who is it?'

'My dear Monsieur Clements, I am not at liberty to name names. But set yourself at ease - the person to whom I refer will very soon be apprehended. Then you will know all.'

Louis could feel beads of perspiration forming on his brow. Fervently and maliciously he hoped that both the poisonous and ineffectual Peterkin and his contact in the household would indeed fall into the clutches of the law, and be harshly dealt with. His arms and shoulders ached, and his hands were growing numb.

'My dear sirs, I beg you to untie me,' he said in wheedling tones. 'You will, I am sure, forgive me for attempting to strike you. I could not be sure who you were, you see. You could have been – *de l'autre cote.'*

'Oh, yes,' said Max, nodding wisely. 'Of course. I see that now.'

'I say, Monsieur, would you care for a brandy? We were just about to have one. Oh, do untie him, Max.' Guy wandered over to the sideboard. 'You know, I'm awfully glad none of us took off our braces – wouldn't that have been embarrassing, when we found out who you were?'

Max helped their guest to am armchair; Guy handed him a brandy. 'Cigar? Cigarette? Yes, do, please. They're Alexandrian.'

'Tell me,' began Max, his eyes fixed on their

guest's face, 'Monsieur - oh I'm sorry, I don't know your name? I'm Max Fareham, by the way, and this is Guy Clements. But you know that already, of course.'

The man inclined his head politely. 'Charmed, Monsieur Fareham. But just call me Louis. No fuller names are advisable, in my profession.'

'Well, Monsieur - Louis,' went on Max, 'How do you know Mr Holmes? I mean, how did you come to be working together?'

'Ah.' Louis sipped his brandy and swirled it gently, feeling a pleasant tingle as the circulation returned to his hand. He puffed on his cigarette for a moment, narrowing his eyes thoughtfully.

'It was the winter of '83. I was in St Petersburg, at the court of the Tsar; Monsieur Holmes was there also, sent by the Government to - well, let's just say that we worked together with considerable success. *'Louis,'* he said to me after the death of the terrible Ivanovitch, *'Louis, you have served our cause well, and I shall mention your name to the Premier in my despatch'*. But tut -' Louis lowered his gaze deprecatingly, 'I speak of what I should not. In my profession, it is unwise to boast of our triumphs. Our failures, alas, usually have consequences too dreadful to conceal.'

'Gosh,' said Guy, 'It sounds awfully dangerous!'

'Well,' Louis lowered his eyes again, 'One gets used to danger.' He looked up keenly. 'But we depend upon the discretion of gentlemen such as your good selves. I shall tell Monsieur Holmes of your actions tonight. He will be full of admiration, I'm sure.'

He extracted his fobwatch, examined it with careful surprise, and swallowed the rest of his brandy. 'Indeed, I have a rendezvous with him shortly! My dear young friends, I thank you for your forbearance, your brandy, and this excellent cigarette. It is time for me to return to my duties.'

He rose, and straightened his clothing. This was the crucial moment. If his bluff failed now ...

Guy retrieved his hat, which had rolled into a corner. 'Here you are sir,' he said, handing it to him.

Max held out his revolver carefully. 'You'd better take this back sir,' he said; 'Er - will you leave by the front door, or would you prefer -?'

'But yes, the main door if I may.' Louis moved towards the passage, and allowed himself to be ushered along it and out into freedom.

'Do give our regards to Mr Holmes, won't you?' said Max as they shook hands on the top step. 'And go carefully - it's starting to rain.'

'But of course. *Adieu, Messieurs!'*

'Bonne chance,' called Guy gaily as their visitor skipped nimbly down the steps and disappeared into the night.

She did not attempt to struggle further. There was no way out of the passage except through the front door, now closed. She supposed the game was up, and in a distant way she regretted that. Mikey was well out if it, though. She'd die before she betrayed Mikey.

She guessed they didn't know about the jewels, hidden against her skin; and being toffs, they probaby wouldn't search her. Maybe they didn't know all that much - but no, he'd just called her by her name, hadn't he? The last minute was already a confusion of panic in her mind. She should have scarpered as soon as she'd had that prickly feeling turning into the street; she'd thought it was just because she felt vulnerable out of disguise. Her mouth set angrily in a line of ivory. Shaken she was, but the adrenalin in her blood made her feel hot and light. Just keep your wits about you, she told herself firmly as they entered Louis' room.

It looked exactly as usual. She half expected to see Mister Louis in that armchair.

'Please, sit down,' said Mr Sherlock Holmes.

The other one led her to the couch and sat near her. He was a nice-looking man, she noted; soft, maybe. Holmes locked the door; she heard the key turn.

'Are you hurt, young lady?' asked the soft one with concern.

She looked down at herself; her hands, wrists and

the front of her dress were bloody. She smiled slowly. 'It's not mine, mister. Better ask your friend.'

'It's nothing.' Holmes was sitting in Louis' armchair, leaning forward and holding his wrist tightly. His shirt cuff was crimson.

'Hurts, does it Mister?' she jeered. He said nothing, but she thought he looked very white.

'Holmes?' asked his friend.

'Just lend me your handkerchief, Watson.'

She watched impassively as he bound it tightly round his hand. It was stained in a moment, but he ignored it.

'Now then,' he said, 'I believe we've met before, young lady. At Mr Guy Clements' house.'

She looked at him sardonically. 'So? Is that a good reason to assault a respectable girl? I can tell you, Mr Sherlock Holmes, I intend to lodge a complaint about this. My character can stand it.'

She watched his face as she spoke. It was a threadbare ruse, but she could at least gauge the extent of his knowledge. The grey eyes met hers, and she sensed a keenness of wit to match her own. And there was something else - the lean face held not a hint of anger.

'Indeed,' he said quietly, 'I very much regret the roughness of your reception. I hope you will accept my apologies.'

She narrowed her eyes. What was all this? Was he soft, too?

'Well, I think I'm owed an explanation. I'm not used to *ungentlemanly behaviour*.' She emphasised the words. 'And I was forced to defend myself, wasn't I, through being took by surprise. I've a right to self defence, I suppose, same as any lady?'

'Yes.'

'Oh, good. Thank you so much!' She heard her own voice sounding harsh and common. She raged inwardly.

'Do you have any objection to my smoking, Miss Peterson?' he asked. She studied him for irony; there was none.

'I'll have one of those, then, if you don't mind. I suppose you can spare it.' She half smiled at his surprise.

'Think I shouldn't?' Her lip curled, but he leaned across, handed her a cigarette and lit it for her.

'You are an unusual woman,' he said.

'You bet.' (Get round him like that? She glanced at the soft one, then back at Holmes. No. No chance. So that was something.) She held the cigarette carefully between her small fingers. She looked at her hands.

'I want to wash this off, Mister,' she said.

Holmes smiled. 'So do I. But we must both wait, I'm afraid. Come,' he went on in a serious tone, 'We have little time. I am sorry, Miss Peterson, but I must shortly place you in the custody of Scotland Yard.'

She blew a cloud of smoke into the space between them.

'Hear him?' she said, addressing Watson. 'Cocky, isn't he?' Watson looked back at her sadly, and she shifted her gaze. Soft. 'Go on then. Tell me why,

Mister, and then I'll tell you why not.'

Holmes sighed. 'You have been passing official documents to a foreign agent who lives at this address,' he said with an almost regretful air. She laughed.

'Oh, is that all? And how does a respectable housemaid like me get hold of official documents?'

His eyes were focussed on a point a little above her head. He spoke abstractedly.

'Your brother Michael, like many other young men of his looks and background, makes a living upon the streets. In the course of his work, he is in a position to steal, deceive and blackmail. At some point in your young lives you've devised a system for utilising his gains and his knowledge, and have no doubt built up an efficient network of contacts. An employee of the War Office was the latest victim of this enterprise, and through this unfortunate you gained hold of certain papers. How you made the acquaintance of Louis la Rothière is of little importance; what *is* of interest is that you, showing remarkable courage and ingenuity, have been visiting him in the guise of a young man. You have already sold him one set of papers; the others you secreted at the house of your employer, in a vase in the drawing room.'

He lowered his eyes to meet hers. 'Both of these documents are now in my possession. Monsieur La Rothière, I believe, is currently in the hands of the police. You, meanwhile, having been made aware of my investigation into the matter, wisely decided against going home tonight. Whether you've made any attempt to retrieve the papers from Mr Clements' residence I do not yet know; but you've just taken the risk of visiting La Rothière undisguised, either to explain matters, to ask for help, or to exhort money. I trust I have omitted no point of importance?'

She ground her cigarette end into the carpet beneath her heel.

'You're mad,' she said clearly. 'It's a pack of lies. I don't know what Louis does for a living, and I don't care. He's been good to me, that's all. I visit him occasionally, yes, and we have a nice time. Nothing unusual in that, eh?'

She looked contemptuously at Holmes. 'You've got nothing but daydreams to pin on me, Mister. All right, so I need to earn a little money on the side. What's it to do with you? Pure as the driven yourself, are you?'

Holmes shrugged. 'I do not believe there is any advantage in debating the matter; I can gather the necessary evidence. It will save time if you speak to me now, that's all.'

'And if Louis *did* ask me to look after some things for him,' went on Madeleine, 'I'm not to know what they are, am I? I'm not educated like you.'

She smiled faintly. 'Your posh talk has got me all confused. You can see how he's trying to confuse me, can't you?' She turned to Watson. 'First he tries to assault me, now he's using his posh talk to frighten me. I'm just a poor girl trying to scrape a living. Got a poor, sick mother to care for. As for my brother, well it's come as a dreadful shock, what you just told me. Our mother won't never get over it. That must be why he's gone and done a runner - been worried sick about him, I have.'

She smiled almost pleasantly at Watson. 'See what I mean? And d'you think I could pass for a boy? Wouldn't take *you* in for a minute, would I? Oh, no. And this clever spy never knew? Blind and deaf, is he? Come off it, Mr Clever Dick. You let me go, and I'll drop the charge of assault.'

Holmes rose and stood before her. He looked down at the small figure coiled tense as a steel spring on the edge of the sofa.

'You are a brave and resourceful young woman, Miss Peterson,' he said simply. 'I almost hope the jury will believe you. But the outcome is not mine to predict. Come, Watson, escort this young lady to the door while I fetch a cab.'

Holmes crossed the room, unlocked the door and walked out into the passage. Madeleine heard him loosen the bolts of the front door, felt the draught of cool air waft into the house.

Watson rose and offered her his arm. She took it, and they stepped into the hallway. The front door stood open. She could see Holmes' tall figure beneath the street lamp, and the first drops of rain falling through its yellow light.

As they approached the threshold, she appeared to stumble. 'Hang on, Mister - my shoe -' she said, stooping to adjust it. Watson stepped out onto the doorstep, blocking the entrance and watching her keenly. With the speed of thought she sprang forward, slammed the heavy door in his face and shot one of the big bolts home.

She leant for a moment against the wood, hearing the hammering outside and the hammering of her heart; then she sped back along the dim passageway, hurled herself across the room where they'd been sitting and heaved up the sash of the back window. She straddled the windowsill and made a quick sweep of the scene below: a side wall ran the length of the garden, giving access to the back of the terrace; the drop to it was steep, but a fruit tree grew beside it, strong and mature with branches reaching out towards the sill. Rain pattered in its leaves as she leapt, grappled, dropped, ran, and scrambled up and over.

Seconds later she was in the back alley, her heart thumping against the jewels in her bosom as she threaded her way between houses as sure and nimble as a cat.

'I really don't see how things could have turned out worse!' Sherlock Holmes declared as Watson dabbed the jagged gash on his hand with a carbolised pad.

'This will need a stitch or two, Holmes. Thank heavens the tendon is unharmed. You won't be playing the violin for a while, though.' Watson turned to fetch his black bag from the table.

It was eight o'clock in the morning, and he'd only just persuaded Holmes to let him examine the wound properly. They'd spent hours with Lestrade at the Yard, hours scouring wet streets for the girl before that; or so it seemed to Watson. He was dead beat. His face, when he caught sight of it in the mirror, looked slack and grey. He crossed back to the window.

Holmes was sitting with his back to the light, smoking cigarette after cigarette and sipping occasionally at the strong, scalding coffee Mrs Hudson had brought up. He'd been complaining incessantly for the last half-hour.

'It's not the girl that bothers me, Watson. Don't think that. If we didn't have the wit to prevent her escape then she deserves her freedom. Ouch!'

'Just keep still, my dear fellow,' murmured the Doctor as he gently tautened the thread. 'It won't take a moment.'

'Although I must say,' continued Holmes bitterly,

'it was a somewhat transparent ruse - ouch! For God's sake, Watson, just leave it alone. No, it's that confounded spy. *How* did he get past Lestrade's man? I might have known their inefficiency would bungle everything. And that idiot of a constable actually watched him leave! By the front door, if you please! Shown out with fond farewells by your ridiculous friends! For pity's sake, Watson, haven't you finished *yet*?'

'Just keep still, can't you?' said Watson. He began to bandage the hand.

'Anyway, we've seen the last of La Rothière. Really, the whole case has been a fiasco from beginning to end. You know nothing depresses me more than failure. Perhaps I should give up the whole business. I'm losing my grip, Watson; I shall be no better than Lestrade soon.'

Watson glanced up at his friend. His face was dead white, the eyes deeply shadowed, and he looked miserable. He ground the stub of his cigarette viciously into the coffee saucer. 'Have you finished *now*?' he snapped.

'Quite,' said Watson, packing up his bag. 'Try not to strain that hand for a few days. And I prescribe a good long sleep. You need rest, my dear fellow. Then you'll be able to see things in proportion.'

Holmes snorted rudely, and ran his good hand roughly through his hair. 'How can I sleep, when both my quarries have slipped the net? Did you see Lestrade's face? He was positively gloating.'

'But you retrieved the documents, Holmes. That in

itself was a successful outcome, surely?' Watson helped himself to a slice of cold toast, and reached for the marmalade. 'Eat something now, there's a good fellow. You had no dinner last night, remember.'

Watson too had gone without dinner, though Scotland Yard's duty officer had brought him a ham and pickle sandwich and a mug of tea at three in the morning. Holmes, of course, had taken nothing.

'I am shamed,' went on Holmes angrily. 'I will go down in the annals of detection as a fool and bungler. Take it from me, Watson, this is what comes of allowing one's emotions to cloud the issue. I felt sorry for the girl; that was an unpardonable weakness.'

'Holmes,' said Watson quietly, 'Please eat something. And calm down.'

In answer, Holmes pushed away his coffee and began to pace the room. Watson sighed loudly, and was about to speak again when the bell rang downstairs.

'Ha, news for us!' barked Holmes, hastily smoothing his hair as he turned towards the door.

'But what's he going to *say*, Maxy?' whispered Guy.

'For the thousandth time, I don't *know*', hissed Max.

They were standing on the doorstep of 221B Baker Street, both hollow-eyed and pale. Guy rarely stirred before ten, and it was something of a feat for him to be abroad at eight. He fingered his necktie nervously.

'Do I look all right?' he asked; Max was about to say 'No!' in exasperation when Mrs Hudson opened the door.

'Is Mr Holmes in, Mrs Hudson?' asked Max nervously; 'I know it's early, but -'

'Go straight up,' she said with a complete lack of interest.

They mounted the stairs, knocked at the door and received a peremtory request to enter.

Mr Holmes was standing in the middle of the room looking eagerly towards them. He was wearing his dressing gown; his clothes beneath had a rather crumpled appearance. His right hand was swathed in a bandage, and his face was pale and strained.

Dr Watson was seated at the table. He motioned them in, waving a piece of toast.

'Hello, my dear fellows,' he said pleasantly. 'Come in, come in. You find us just returned from a long night's work, so please excuse our appearance.'

He did indeed look tired and worn, but his voice was as warm as ever. They picked their way into the smoke-laden room, stepping over a crumpled heap of gutted newspapers and a pot of glue. Holmes waved them towards the couch, and went to lean against the mantelpiece. It was evident that they were not the visitors he'd been hoping for; his look was cold and critical. Max dropped his eyes quickly.

Guy's reaction to perceived disapproval was always to turn on the charm. Max watched him assume the look of helpless appeal usually reserved for tutors and rich relatives.

'Oh Mr Holmes,' he gushed, 'We have such dreadful news! It really is too embarrassing, after all you've done for us, but it definitely wasn't our fault this time. After all, he *was* one of your colleagues. But maybe he didn't realise what we'd agreed. Did he make it to the rendezvous in time?'

Holmes picked up a pipe from the mantelpiece and began to fill it slowly, left-handed, regarding Guy with a mixture of curiosity and annoyance.

'Would it be too much to ask you to express yourself clearly and succinctly, Mr Clements?' he asked; 'I believe you have a certain amount of explaining to do, and I am really in no mood to -'

'Some coffee?' offered Dr Watson quickly. 'I daresay you need it. You both look rather shocked.'

'Oh, Dr Watson,' said Guy in a pained voice, 'I would be so grateful. I haven't had any breakfast, and hardly any sleep at all.'

'Thank you, Dr Watson,' said Max glumly. He could not think why Mr Holmes was being so unfriendly, but he could see that he'd lost the admiration won from him yesterday, and that Guy's charm was not having the desired effect.

Holmes turned away with an impatient gesture while Watson quietly provided coffee for their visitors, chatting gently as he did so about the stimulating effects of the beverage after a long night. He pointedly placed a fresh cup beside Holmes' armchair, and directed by his meaningful gaze Holmes finally sat down.

'Have you hurt yourself, sir?' asked Max tentatively.

'No. Now, perhaps you'd care to tell me why you were entertaining a notorious spy at your residence last night, Mr Clements,' said Holmes grimly.

'Oh, we knew he was a spy,' said Guy airily. 'He told us all about the time you worked together at the Russian Court and defeated Ivan the Terrible. But I don't think he realised that *I* was supposed to give back the diamonds. That's why we're here. Has he given them to you?'

Holmes held up a hand to stop the flow.

'Please, Mr Clements.' He looked at Max. 'Would you care to translate for me, Mr Fareham?'

Guy pouted, and Max began hurriedly. 'Last night when we got home, we found a man called Louis in Guy's drawing room. We didn't know who he was, so we jumped him -'

'And sat on him. *I* sat on him.'

'And I took his gun -'

' - which wasn't loaded, because he said he just -'

'Please, Guy. And he said that he worked for the

Government and they'd sent him to retrieve the plans, but he didn't realise that you already had them. He was French. And he said you and he had worked together in the past -'

'Against Ivan the Terrible!'

'-yes, and that he had a rendezvous with you, and he was glad you had the papers ... oh. He was lying, wasn't he, Mr Holmes?'

Max's worst suspicions were confirmed by the look on Holmes' face. His voice faltered, and he bit his lip.

'But you've left out the most important thing!' shouted Guy, bouncing on the edge of his chair. In his impatience he'd completely missed the nuances of Holmes' expression, and the conclusion of Max's speech.

'After he left, I looked for the diamonds - Max had put them in the vase, where the papers were - and they *weren't there*! They'd gone! And he was one of your agents! Well, not one of *your* agents, but one of, you know, *them*. He said you're one too. So did he bring them to you? If not, could you tell him that *I* was supposed to do all the returning and explaining, and - well, *I* don't think it's funny.'

Mr Holmes had started to laugh. He continued laughing until he was breathless, and Dr Watson joined him, much to their astonishment.

'Oh dear, oh dear!' said Watson when he could speak. 'My poor boys! You see, Holmes, we're not the only bunglers in this city. This would make a pretty case for *The Strand*.'

'I beg of you, my dear fellow,' gasped Holmes, 'Do

not, if you value your life, write up an account of this. My practice would fail overnight. Ah, dear ...'

He pulled himself together and faced their visitors. 'I apologise for my laughter, and for my ill-temper. I'm hardly in a position to blame you for your mistake; you at least caught and disarmed your villain before letting him go, while ours not only managed to stab me but escaped our custody with ease.'

Guy looked at Max aghast.

'So he wasn't a friend of yours, Mr Holmes? He was a villain after all? But he said - he said I'd been harbouring a desperate spy in my household. He was ever so convincing.'

'Of course he was,' nodded Holmes, now completely sober. 'Louis La Rothière is an accomplished impersonator; he goes by many names, and several nationalities I believe. I'm very sorry to hear that he escaped with your mother's diamonds, however. That is most unfortunate. The police are watching the ports for him, but to be frank I'm not overly hopeful. He is a resourceful rogue, and a master of disguise.'

Guy's mouth remained open in dismay.

'Oh. Oh! So Mother's lost her diamonds all over again? That's awful! But it wasn't me this time, so I don't have to confess, do I? Do you think, Mr Holmes, that you could just, you know, just tell her that a notorious spy took them?'

'But who was the villain who escaped your custody?' asked Max curiously. He was sure that the matter of Guy's filial explanations would be better sorted out later, when Mr Holmes was less tired.

'Ah,' said Holmes with a wry smile. 'You'll be surprised to hear that the desperate spy you've been harbouring unawares, the daring and ruthless villain who got the better of us last night, was none other than Madeleine Peterson. Your housemaid, Mr Clements.'

He was watching their faces; Guy's was blank. 'Madeleine Peterson?' he repeated.

'I think you knew her as Mary. Your mother obviously prefers plain names for the family servants.'

Guy's eyes widened in disbelief. *'Mary?* What, the one who lived out? That Mary?'

'Even she.'

The concept was obviously difficult for Guy to grasp. 'What, she - but how could she - was she working for that Frenchman, then? Was she *planted* in my household? Do you know, I never liked her. She was different from the others. Insolent. I said so, didn't I Max? Was it her who put the plans in my vase? What incredible cheek! Right under my nose, too! Well, it just goes to show, doesn't it, that we're none of us safe in our own houses!'

'She was not *planted*, Mr Clements,' said Holmes calmly. 'She was working on her own initiative, aided and abetted by her younger brother Michael - a boy who by all accounts bears a certain resemblance to yourself. He makes his living on the streets, and obtained the plans from one of his clients. He handed them over to his sister to hide while she negotiated a price with Monsieur Louis La Rothière.'

Max, although scarcely less shocked than Guy, was quick to piece the evidence together.

'So *that's* why you suspected Guy! If this brother resembles him, I mean.'

Holmes nodded. 'Precisely. And Miss Peterson has now got the better of us all. I doubt whether she's turned up for work today, Clements! I have been thwarted in my investigations by an uneducated girl - and prevented from practising my violin for some time to come.' He waved his bandaged hand. 'But at least the plans are safe, and should by now have been returned to the War Office. Lady Esher's fake diamonds may be on their way out of the country however ... and I'd rather not contemplate the damage to my reputation.'

'But Mr Holmes,' said Max earnestly, 'Why did you not have Guy's house watched, if you suspected one of his servants?'

Holmes sighed. 'You're quite right, my dear Fareham. I was labouring under the misapprehension that the house *was* being watched. However, it seems the Yard had several projects in hand, and the constable who was supposed to raise the alarm had not been properly briefed.' He shrugged. 'The whole thing has been something of a debacle.'

Guy wriggled impatiently. 'This is all very well,' he said petulantly, 'but what am I to say to Mother? She won't believe me in a million years if I tell her that I pawned them, and got them back, and then had a spy in for drinks one evening who took them instead of some top secret documents!'

'Guy,' said Max warningly, 'All this can wait …'

'No, it's all right Mr Fareham. I do appreciate your position, Mr Clements, and I'd rather you said nothing to you mother, or indeed to anyone else, about any spies or secret documents if you don't mind.'

'I could have my allowance cut off!' wailed Guy. 'I'm not supposed to consort with bad types, and I'm sure French spies would come under that heading.'

'Mr Clements! I was about to suggest that you leave the matter in my hands. I'm not convinced, mark you, that a full confession to your mother would not do you a deal of good, but under the circumstances I think I had better see to it. After all, it's still just possible that they may be recovered.'

'Oh Mr Holmes, thankyou *so* much.' Guy looked greatly relieved. He smiled sweetly and ingratiatingly at Holmes as he watched him light his pipe.

'Did you say something about coffee, Watson?' murmured Holmes between puffs.

'It's by your chair, my dear fellow,' said the Doctor, 'Though I suspect it will be cold by now.'

'Well ring for a fresh pot, will you, and some toast and eggs too if you can brave Mrs Hudson for a second time … would you care for some breakfast, Mr Fareham? Mr Clements? Of course you would. Now tell me - *what* am I supposed to have been doing in Russia with Louis la Rothierè?'

'It wasn't too bad after all, was it?' said Max as they walked home. 'I thought we were in terrible trouble, the way he looked at us at first.'

'So did I! But then I turned on the charm - did you notice? - and he soon softened up. I do think, Maxy, that we should invite them round for dinner some time. Just to say thankyou.'

'It's a wonderful idea, but - I don't think he'd come.'

Max sighed. He knew that in Mr Holmes' eyes he and Guy were just two foolish boys who'd caused a great deal of nuisance. He hoped - it was disloyal to Guy, but he couldn't help it - he hoped that he might be the more favoured of the two ... but it was unlikely, most unlikely, that Mr Holmes would want to see him socially. Better not to send an invitation at all than to suffer the pain of a rebuff.

They were sauntering through the park. Last night's rain had cleared the air a little, but the day was still set to be humid. Max found himself beginning to pine for the countryside. He longed to unstring himself, to let himself down and just be quiet for a while; to sit perfectly still, and have Guy sit perfectly still with him. As they passed beneath the dark, green hands of a horse-chestnut, he took his friend's arm and drew him into the damp-smelling shade.

'Guy,' he said.

'What?'

'Let's go away together.'

'What, elope, you mean?'

'Don't be silly. A holiday. A holiday together somewhere.'

Guy narrowed his eyes suspiciously. 'Paris, Max. You promised me Paris, and I utterly refuse to be deflected from that goal.'

Max sighed. He bid a regretful farewell to his vision of green fields and stillness. 'All right then. Paris. Just you and I. We'll stroll along the Bois de Boulogne and forget all about spies and Government papers and fake diamonds and ... just be ourselves.'

Guy looked into Max's golden-brown eyes and said, 'Max Fareham, if you don't take me home this instant I shall kiss you right here.'

'Then we'd get run in, and even Mr Holmes wouldn't be able to help us.'

'Oh, I don't know,' drawled Guy, steering him gently back towards the path; 'Mr Holmes can do anything if he sets his mind to it. You know, Maxy, I've come to agree with you. He *is* wonderful. You were right all along.'

Louis la Rothière was in philosophical mode. He sighed thoughtfully as he adjusted the new kid gloves on his manicured hands; they were a little tight still, but one had to protect oneself from the grime of a railway journey. He looked out of the window at wide green fields, dotted here and there with fat cattle and low stone outbuildings; the leisurely, bland decorum of the French countryside. At least here there'd be no risk of encountering Mr Sherlock Holmes!

How galling, though, to have come away empty-handed from what had promised to be such a lucrative enterprise. He could not rid himself of the impression that somewhere along the way he'd missed a vital piece of the jigsaw ... galling, in the extreme. He supposed that the papers concealed at his former lodgings must by now be back with the War Office. Ah, well - no use crying over spilt milk, as his mother used to say. One made mistakes, it was true, but when one door closed another always opened. Time to move on.

Paris would be pleasant for a few months. Of course he would not attempt to pass as a Frenchman there! *Mr Herbert Dutton* was the name on his passport, freshly provided by his Embassy contact. It came with strings attached, naturally - it would be irksome, having to report to a paymaster again after sampling the delights of independence - but who knew what interesting little sidelines and opportunities Paris might have to offer?

Louis opened a small silver case, took out a cigar, and lit it carefully. Mr Herbet Dutton – a dealer in antiques, travelling to France on business. He'd have some cards printed as soon as he reached his destination.

He sat back in his seat and stretched out his legs. The world, he thought, was his oyster. He blew a cloud of smoke towards the carriage roof, and smiled.

*****

ACKNOWLEDGEMENTS

Heartfelt thanks to the following whose generosity, help and encouragement have enabled me to bring this long overdue baby to birth: Jayne Raven, Magenta Wise, Gregory Nelson, The Retired Beekeepers of Sussex (specifically Katie Alexander, Basil Chap and Elinor Gray), and last but never least my own partner in crime, Leslie Bunker.

Rohase Piercy was born in London in 1958, and now lives in Brighton on the South Coast of England with her husband Leslie and dog Spike. She has two grown-up daughters.

Also by Rohase Piercy

My Dearest Holmes

The Coward Does It With A Kiss

Before Elizabeth

For Children:
What Brave Bulls Do
(Illustrated by Nina Falaise)

Printed in Poland
by Amazon Fulfillment
Poland Sp. z o.o., Wrocław